## "I'll be in touch," Nora said as she walked away

She started for the gate, then doubled back, realizing she ought to give him a business card.

"Thank you." He accepted the card and their fingers brushed. The contact was minute, but it was enough to send an electric zap down the length of her arm. She yanked her hand back and the corner of his mouth lifted in subtle acknowledgment. She eyed him suspiciously. Had he felt it, too?

But he offered nothing, saying "I look forward to hearing your ideas," before ascending the front steps and disappearing into the house.

Nora stared down at her fingers, all too aware of her physical reaction to Ben's brief touch. Grimacing, she wiped her hand on the back of her jeans and stalked to her truck. She'd never been the type to act all fluttery and girly over a guy. Wasn't her style.

Nora glowered at the house, more specifically at Ben inside, and jerked her truck into gear. Not gonna happe

Dear Reader,

If you're just finding the Emmett's Mill series and by proxy the Simmons sisters, you're in for a wild ride with Nora. I'll confess she was my favorite character, as she says and does what she feels is appropriate at the moment and deals with the aftermath later. But even as Nora has been accused of being acerbic and abrasive at times (which I cannot deny) it doesn't take a forensic scientist to discern that Nora hides a generous heart underneath all that bluster. Much like her father, Gerald.

If you've been following the series, you already know (and probably love) the youngest Simmons sister. She's no shrinking violet and she gives as good as she gets. Benjamin Hollister III is everything Nora doesn't like about people from the city. Aloof, condescending and arrogant, Ben rubs Nora the wrong way. Too bad they share a history—one that includes the memory of a first kiss, which has never quite faded.

I've loved writing about the sisters. As the oldest of three myself, I know a thing or two about the female dynamic. There's a mysterious bond that tethers women of the same family and while sometimes we might strain at the bond, other times it is our lifeline.

Please enjoy Nora and Ben's story, and keep a lookout for the story of Dean Halvorsen, the oldest of the Halvorsen brothers, coming late fall of 2008. Hearing from readers is one of the highlights of my day. Feel free to drop me a line anytime. You can write me at P.O. Box 2210, Oakdale, CA 95361, or at author@kimberlyvanmeter.com.

Happy reading,

*Kimberly Van Meter*

# A KISS TO REMEMBER
*Kimberly Van Meter*

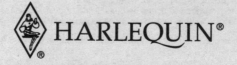

TORONTO • NEW YORK • LONDON
AMSTERDAM • PARIS • SYDNEY • HAMBURG
STOCKHOLM • ATHENS • TOKYO • MILAN • MADRID
PRAGUE • WARSAW • BUDAPEST • AUCKLAND

ISBN-13: 978-0-373-78230-7
ISBN-10:    0-373-78230-6

A KISS TO REMEMBER

www.eHarlequin.com

**Printed in U.S.A.**

## ABOUT THE AUTHOR

An avid reader since before she can remember, Kimberly Van Meter started her writing career at 16 when she finished her first novel, typing late nights and early mornings on her mother's old portable typewriter. Although that first novel was nothing short of literary mud, with each successive piece of work her writing improved to the point of reaching that coveted published status.

Kimberly, now a journalist, and her husband and three kids make their home in Oakdale. She enjoys writing, reading, photography and drinking hot chocolate by the windowsill when it rains.

**Books by Kimberly Van Meter**

**HARLEQUIN SUPERROMANCE**
1391—THE TRUTH ABOUT FAMILY
1433—FATHER MATERIAL
1469—RETURN TO EMMETT'S MILL

To my three most perfect creations—
Sebastian, Jaidyn and Eryleigh. I am so blessed
the universe chose me as your mother.
You make me proud every day.

To my growing list of loyal readers.
Without you, I'd be no one.

To my publisher and editor for believing in me.
I'm forever grateful.

And to my agent, Pam,
for her patience and vision.

# CHAPTER ONE

NORA SIMMONS DROVE past the old Victorian that sat on the outskirts of Emmett's Mill as she went on her way to Sonora to meet with a prospective client, and what she saw made her stomp on the brakes and nearly eat her steering wheel.

A sleek, shiny black import convertible sports car sat in the driveway, completely out of place for the aging home with its chrome wheels and leather interior, parked as if it had a right to be there when it certainly did not.

*Sonofabitch trespassers.* She made a quick U-turn, kicking up dirt and gravel as her truck chewed up some of the shoulder and barreled toward the house. Whoever it was, they weren't local. Nora was willing to bet her eyeteeth on that score. No one in Emmett's Mill drove a BMW roadster, as far as she knew—a car like that would stick out in the little community. Driving such a hot little number around town was likely to drop jaws and send a lot of die-hard American-manufacturer purists shaking their heads in disgust. For a town in California, Emmett's Mill had a peculiar attitude at times.

She hopped from her truck with her cell phone in case the sheriff was needed and prowled for the trespasser, caution at approaching a stranger barely registered. She was sick of tourists thinking that just because the town was small and quaint, the locals enjoyed having their privacy invaded. Well, B.J. and Corrinda might be dead, but Nora was not about to let a stranger wander all over their place.

She rounded the side of the expansive house and found an incredibly tall man with fashionably cut blue-black hair, with an air about him that reeked of money and privilege, examining what had at one time been Corrinda Hollister's prized roses.

Nora often found herself looking up at the opposite sex, but the breadth of his frame complemented this man's height, creating a strong, powerful build that immediately made her feel distinctly feminine. She scowled and silenced the breathless prattle in her head as she stomped toward him, purpose blotting out anything other than her own ire at his trespassing on private property.

"Can I help you?"

He turned, surprised that he wasn't alone, and no doubt the frost in her voice and the annoyed arch of one brow said volumes, as if she were the one who didn't belong on the property. "Excuse me?" he said, giving her a hard look from eyes so green they almost looked fake.

The breath caught in her throat as she met his gaze. Swallowing against the very real sensation of déjà vu, she continued in a strident tone that betrayed little of what she felt inside. "I said, can I help you? In case you weren't aware, most people don't take kindly to strangers parking in their driveway and trespassing." His perturbed expression egged her on and she launched into him with fresh vengeance. "I happen to know the people who used to live here so don't try to say something like they were friends of yours or some other kind of bull puckey. I'll tell you what…if you just get back in your fancy car and get off the property I won't call the sheriff. Fair enough?"

"Your Mayberry Neighborhood Watch routine is cute but not necessary. I own this house."

What nerve. "Nice try, but I happen to know different," she retorted, ignoring the faint glimmer of something at the back of her brain and continuing indignantly. "This house belonged to—"

"B.J. and Corrinda Hollister, up until six months ago when they both died in an unfortunate car accident, leaving the house to their only grandson. Me."

The air left her lungs. Ben? She stared a little harder and although she didn't want to see it, that niggling glimmer crystallized in her memory and the image of a boy she'd kissed one summer changed into the strong facial planes of the man watching her sternly.

*Oh shiza.* "You're Ben Hollister?"

"It's the name on my birth certificate."

She took in the shoulders that filled his dark Henley and hinted at the solid swell of muscle hidden underneath, and the spit dried in her mouth. Where was the skinny twelve-year-old kid with braces and his hair falling over one eye? Who was this *man?*

He turned away, dismissing her again and all she could think to say was a lame "No, you're not."

He did an annoyed double take. "I am and this is becoming irritating. Who the hell are *you?*"

She was about to jog his memory, but something—pride mainly—made her stop.

She didn't consider herself a great beauty—not that she didn't catch her fair share of men looking her way—but most people said her personality made her hard to forget.

She sent him a suspicious look, but his only response was an increasingly testy glare. Either he truly didn't recognize her or he was a fabulous actor. To be fair, she looked as different as he did when they were kids. Too bad Nora wasn't in a gracious mood.

"Well, are you going to tell me who you are or not? If not, you know your way out."

Temptation to spin on her heel and do exactly that had her toes twitching but she wanted to see his reaction when she revealed her identity. Surely, her name—if not her appearance—would strike a chord, and when that burst of recognition went off like a paparazzi camera flash, she'd unleash the windstorm he'd earned for neglecting his grandparents over the years. For God's sake, the man skipped out on their funeral and now he was here surveying the property as if it were a spoil of war? What an asshole.

"Listen, I—"

"Nora Simmons," she cut in, waiting for that delicious reaction to cue her next comment, which after years of practice, had become rather scathing. But he offered very little for her to grab on to. The momentary glimmer in his eyes didn't blossom into full-blown acknowledgment as she'd hoped, but winked out in a blink and his next question was like a lawn mower over her ego.

"You're the landscape architect who did the gardens at Senator Wilkinson's lakeside estate? Near Bass Lake?" He accepted her slow nod with a smug grin that showcased each of his pearly-white, braces-free teeth, and she could only stare warily. He continued, completely missing her confusion. "How synchronistic. I was planning to call you later in the week. I never imagined you might come charging in like the Neighborhood Watch brigade, but it saves me the time of tracking you down."

Uh. What? "I…" *Twilight Zone* episode? *Punk'd?* Something wasn't right. "Wait a minute. Are you saying you don't remember me?"

"Should I?" He gave her a blank expression that looked a little too earnest to be believable and her brain started to bubble.

What game was he playing? She eyed him guardedly, deciding to see where he was going with this. "Uh, never mind. Yes, I worked on Jerry's lake house. Fun project. So, you were saying?"

"Right. I would like to hire you to fix up this place."

It was the way he said *this place* that almost ruined her ability to keep her temper in check, but her curiosity was greater than her desire to pummel him into the ground for his insensitivity, so she made an effort to cast a quick look around the craggy ridge on which the house was perched.

She took in the tall grass, star thistle and twisted branches of manzanita of the surrounding scenery and asked, "What do you mean? What's wrong with it?"

"What's wrong with it?" he repeated incredulously. He pointed at the dead roses and the withered dry grass flanking the house that looked nothing like the beautiful oasis Corrinda had created despite the notoriously hard topsoil that, during the summer, turned to stone without constant tending. In this area of Emmett's Mill it took some skill to grow anything aside from poison oak and manzanita, but Corrinda had coaxed roses and daffodils from the difficult earth.

"Are you kidding me? It's a mess," he said. He turned a speculative eye toward her and she bristled. "Aren't you the best in the area?"

"Some seem to think so." She all but

growled. Thank goodness the Hollisters never saw how their grandson had turned into such a haughty jerk. It would've broken their tender hearts. As it was, the fact that he never returned to Emmett's Mill after that one summer told Nora volumes. Her sister Natalie liked to drone on about not judging people too quickly, but frankly, in Nora's book, if it walks like a duck and quacks like a duck it ain't a giraffe. And right about now, she was thinking Ben Hollister was a jerk. If he wanted to be obtuse, she could be obtuse, too. "What do you want me to fix?"

He gestured toward everything in the yard, from the grass to the bone-dry fountain that looked older than the house itself. "Everything on the outside. Now that I've seen it again, I'll bet the inside isn't much better, but I'll obviously have to hire someone else for that. It's no wonder it hasn't sold. In four months there hasn't been one call. I figured I better come and take a look myself and this is what I find. A broken-down old house with more weeds than dirt that screams 'fixer-upper.'" He turned away and muttered, "I'm going to kill my Realtor for not telling me what I was dealing with."

"You're selling the house?"

He glanced around the yard with a frown.

"It seems the For Sale sign has disappeared. When I call to berate my Realtor about these other issues, I'll be sure to remind her to get another sign out here right away." He looked up to see her staring at him. "Something wrong, Ms. Simmons? You look a little pale."

"You're *selling?*"

"That's what I said. The sign must've disappeared after I had it listed. Some kid probably used it to play mailbox baseball." Nora's continued stare prompted him to ask with a short sigh, "Ms. Simmons…are you hard of hearing? You've been echoing everything I say."

She jerked at his question and the implication that she might be hearing impaired. "No," she answered indignantly. "I'm just surprised, is all."

"Why is that?"

"Because it's your grandparents' house. I would've thought you might like to hang on to it," she said, taking great effort not to clench her teeth.

His black brows furrowed with irritation and her blood pressure peaked as he asked, "Why?"

Why indeed? She refrained from letting sarcasm drip from her voice. "Never mind. My mistake. You were saying? No, I take that back. Why wouldn't you want to keep this beautiful house?"

"Not that it's any of your business, Ms. Simmons, but I plan to use the proceeds from the sale to open my own law practice in the Bay Area. I have no need of a house in the country. I rarely vacation."

He turned away and Nora was struck by a fleeting moment of sadness for a man who never took the time to enjoy what life had to offer. A flash of the boy she'd known for one summer made her wonder where that natural curiosity had gone and why—until she realized she was sympathizing with the enemy and stiffened.

He turned to her, more annoyance on his face. "Are you always so full of questions for your potential clients? I can't say I agree it's a good business practice."

"I don't need business advice from you, thank you," she said, chafing openly at his criticism. "And no, I don't usually care."

Keen interest flared in his eyes but it was gone a heartbeat later. "Why do you care with me?"

"I don't," she answered, not quite convinced she hadn't seen what she'd seen. "I'm just trying to figure out why you'd want to sell the only possession your grandparents owned. Now I know." Subtlety was not her forte, but she was pleased to see her comment rubbed him the wrong way. "Most people I know tend to cherish gifts, especially one with such value."

He'd have to be an idiot not to catch the insult couched inside that seemingly benign statement, but he didn't take the bait as she'd hoped. Instead, he cast a long look around the property, saying, "Well, I can't say much for the Realtor I've listed the house with. I'd have thought as her client she would've told me what I was getting into."

"Who's your Realtor?" she asked for appearances' sake. There were two in Emmett's Mill and only one was female.

"Janelle—" he paused, searching his memory for her name "—Grafton, failed to tell me what a hard sell this was going to be. I figure by hiring you, a local landscape architect, I might create some goodwill and perhaps word of mouth will help move this giant money pit."

"Do you think just because I've grown up in this town once people hear I've done the work on the landscaping the house will sell faster than it would otherwise?"

His mouth twisted. "Of course I do. Two reasons. First, small towns are all about supporting the locals. Second, as I've said, I'm familiar with your work and I know it's good."

"And how is that?"

"How is what?"

"How do you know my work? You mentioned Jerry's lake house and that house is not on my Web site."

He offered a small smile. "I know the right people."

"Yeah? Me, too. I know the sheriff's home number by heart. How'd you know about that job?"

He raised his hands and his mouth tightened. "Calm down. The firm I work for travels in certain political circles. Jerry was bragging about the work you'd done and I was curious, so I started asking around. If it's any consolation, my snooping uncovered only favorable results. Like I said, you do good work. Don't get me wrong. I shopped around and checked other landscape architects, but I kept coming back to you. Your work speaks for itself."

Nora tried not to soften under his praise because, in all honesty, although the words were complimentary, she got the distinct impression they had been delivered with a hint of cynicism. She met his stare. "This isn't

Stars Hollow or Pleasantville or any other fictitious town where everyone is nice and the neighbors bring apple pie when you move to town and the mayor owns a soda shop and holds town meetings in a community garage. You know, it really drives me crazy when people come to a rural area and assume just because we're not choking on smog or rushing to the nearest gourmet coffee shop for some overpriced whipped mocha soy latte with nonfat foam and an organic blueberry muffin, that we're stuck in a time warp. My working on the house won't make a bit of difference. For a lawyer, I gotta tell you, you're A game leaves much to be desired."

"Do you always insult potential clients?"

She smiled. "Not usually. But ordinarily I don't deal with people who have their head up their ass yet have the gall to try to tell me what color the sky is."

The tips of his ears reddened and his gaze hardened. "That will be sufficient, Ms. Simmons. Just because I admire your work doesn't mean I will allow you to continually insult me without provocation."

Nora eyed him with open disdain. "Mr. Hollister, I think we've already established that you need me and not the other way around," she said. "It's no skin off my nose to walk away from this job. Maybe that's what I ought to do. It's obvious you and I don't suit."

A spark flashed in his eyes and a muscle in his jaw twitched, but otherwise there was little to betray what was going on inside his head, which Nora was willing to bet was a maelstrom of pissed-off retaliatory statements. She hadn't meant to say so much, but his arrogance poked at her already roused temper. She was half tempted to tell him exactly why the house wouldn't sell no matter what he did to it, but she wasn't about to give him any kind of advantage.

"Are you finished?"

She hesitated, his civil tone made her leery. Ben struck her as the silent but deadly type. The quieter he got, the more dangerous. "Yeah," she answered.

"Good." He advanced toward her, and for the first time in her life she felt she'd just surrendered the upper hand without even realizing they were in a power struggle. She couldn't take a step back without seeming to be intimidated, but if she didn't put more space between them, she'd be forced to stare up at him, which only made her feel vulnerable and short. Damn her sisters for getting all the height. He was too close; she could smell his expensive cologne and it made her want to lean in for a deeper whiff.

She glared up at him but that was no help, either. In this position she could see the unique flecks of brown woven into the green of his eyes, like freshly turned soil on a grassy hilltop interspersed with flares of gold. She hadn't remembered his eyes being so…gorgeous.

What she did remember was his… Her gaze dropped to his full lips and the slumbering voice of her feminine core whispered in her ear as if awakening from a deep sleep, offering all kinds of torrid suggestions that would make her grandmother blush if not her conscious self. *Ridiculous*, Nora wanted to say. They had been kids, not even old enough to know what they were doing. Why it made such an impression then, and why being so close to him now made her insides quiver and shake was a mystery—one she concluded that was best left unsolved.

His words cut into her thoughts, and although she didn't like what she was hearing, she was immensely grateful for what he said. "You're right. It does seem you and I are not the best fit, but you're the one I want for the job. Your manners stink and you've the professionalism of a hillbilly, but no one can argue that you can create miracles with plants and whatnot. And I think I'm going to need a goddamn miracle to move this house. So, the only thing I want to hear from you is whether or not you'll take the job."

Nora balked and sputtered. Nobody talked to her like that. She had half a mind to sweep his ankle and watch him crash to the ground, but she didn't relish the idea of going to jail for battery.

Her teeth ached as she held back the urge to tell him where he could stick the job, but within the short amount of time she'd been with him, an indescribable lunacy had taken hold of her and she struggled to find stable ground within her own mind. *Think of B.J. and Corrinda,* a desperate voice said, and she clung to it and the accompanying ire. She'd given him the opportunity to exonerate himself from the wretched picture he'd created by bailing on his grandparents, but he'd failed that test miserably. His only motivation for coming here was to sell the one thing his grandparents had owned and left to him with love and hope in their hearts.

The thought burned, but what could she do? She really didn't want someone else to take the job, despite what she may tell Ben. Her gaze threatened to roam the courtyard as her imagination plucked new and exciting ideas from her mental cache, but she held firm. She may tremble with anticipation at getting her hands on this property, but she sure as hell wasn't going to admit it.

*Round one, you namby-pamby, fancy-dressing, loafer-wearing city boy.*

She put her index finger against his chest and gave him a small push to indicate she was back in charge. "I'll take the job, but only if you stay out of my way while I'm doing it."

"I'm your employer. I'll do no such thing. You'll do what I tell you. That's what I'm paying you for."

"You're paying me to fix this house so it will sell. Unless you want to hire someone else, listen to my suggestions."

"God, you're impossible. Has anyone ever told you you're not easy to work with?"

"Nope. All my clients love me."

"I find that hard to believe," he retorted.

"I don't care what you believe. All I care is that your check clears." She turned and deliberately walked away, allowing herself a small victorious smile. He'd learn she wasn't easily bossed, intimidated or impressed. Not even by or with men who were too attractive for their own good. "Meet me here tomorrow. Nineish. We'll discuss details."

He called out to her and she turned but didn't stop walking. "Tomorrow's no good. How about—"

"How about tomorrow?" she interjected, ready to get the hell away from Ben before she did something stupid. She needed to regroup. "Tomorrow's all I got. Take it or leave it."

"You're not the only person in the area I could hire," he snapped, but she simply shrugged as if he could take his chances. She jerked open her truck door and climbed inside. When she looked back at him, he was holding some sort of phone/PDA and moving the stylus in an agitated manner, quickly rescheduling what she assumed were his prior appointments. "Fine, 9:00 a.m. Don't be late," he said, but she was already gunning her engine, loving that the sound drowned out his voice and forced him to yell. "Wait a minute! Do you have a business card or something with a contact phone number?"

"Yep, I sure do." She waved from the truck. "See you tomorrow. Nineish!"

BEN COUGHED as a cloud of dust followed Nora's departure. Ah, hell. He brushed at his fine linen trousers and shirt but still felt the dirt clinging to him. He should've just hired someone else. Someone less difficult. Someone who didn't send odd snaps and sparks arcing through his body when anger caused a dark and dangerous light to flare behind her gray eyes. But someone else wouldn't be the best and that's what he needed. He didn't care what Nora said—he was convinced she was the ticket to selling this house. Her online portfolio was impressive despite the relative obscurity of Emmett's Mill. She had clients all over California. Big, high-profile clients. Her work would move this house faster than some no-name landscape architect who wouldn't argue with him or call him names.

She wasn't the kid he once knew. Except for the name-calling part. That was familiar.

Yeah, he'd lied through his teeth about remembering her but she was far from the kid in his memory. He remembered a honey-haired hoyden with more tangles than curls and a really cute gap-toothed grin that made goofy look cool. She'd been swimming in the creek, her hair had been plastered to her head as if she'd just popped from the water to climb onto the granite slab of rock that descended into the watering hole. When he'd announced his presence, she might've looked guilty for trespassing on private property if it wasn't for the blackberry-juice stain on her lips. If there was ever a picture of a tomboy, she'd fit the bill.

"Who are you?" she'd asked without hesitation, tossing a blackberry into her mouth as if it were a peanut.

"Who are you?" he'd countered, not quite sure what to make of the girl with the wild nest of hair spilling around her bare shoulders. She wore a red string bikini top that covered an area of skin that was as flat as a board and would've taken the imagination of a skilled storyteller to fill and a frayed pair of jean shorts that looked like hand-me-downs from an older sister. His mouth went strangely dry.

"I asked you first."

"I asked you second."

She shrugged and popped the final blackberry in her mouth before hopping to her feet to find more. He had no choice but to follow. She began picking the plump berries, ignoring him completely.

He eyed the tangle of blackberry bushes with fear. "Aren't there snakes?"

She paused and tossed a look over her shoulder. "Probably."

"You're not afraid?"

"My dad says they're more afraid of us than we are of them. As long as I leave them alone, they'll leave me alone. Besides, the only one you gotta worry about is the rattler and they make lots of noise before they bite you."

"What kind of noise?" he asked, straining to listen.

"A *rattling* noise. Duh." She turned and tossed a berry at him. "Here."

"How do you know it's not poisonous?"

The look she gave made him feel as if he was the dumbest person on the planet and he ate it if only to get her to stop looking at him like that. The berry was sweet and juicy and the best thing he'd ever tasted. "I didn't know you could just eat them straight from the bush," he admitted, coming to stand cautiously beside her so he could pick his own.

"Where'd you think they came from?" she asked incredulously.

He shrugged defensively. "I dunno."

"Boy, you're real dumb, you know that?"

"Am not!"

"Anyone who doesn't know where blackberries come from is pretty dumb in my book. You must be a city kid."

The all-knowing tone in her young voice

was all the more degrading because she was right.

"Yeah, so?"

"So, only city kids don't know where their own food comes from. My dad says that you shouldn't be able to eat it if you don't know where it's coming from."

That was a horrifying idea. If that were the case, Ben would most likely starve.

"So who are you?" she asked.

"Ben Hollister," he answered without thought, too focused on the humiliating realization he'd been shown up by some girl. He jerked his head toward the large house on the hill above them. "That's my grandparents' house."

Tinkling laughter followed. "Now I know you're not only dumb but a liar, too. The Hollisters ain't got a grandson."

"Do, too!"

"Do not. I've never seen you before. If you're their grandson, where you been all this time?"

"New England." He lifted his chin, answering with as much disdain as he'd grown up hearing in his father's voice. "You probably don't even know where that's at."

"Wherever it's at, apparently there ain't any blackberry bushes!"

With that, she jumped down from the brambles and skipped toward a bike lying on its side at the water's edge. He scrambled after her.

"Wait! What's your name?" he called after her, intrigued as any twelve-year-old who was alone in a strange town and desperate to make friends—even sass-mouthed girls who made his stomach feel weird—would be. She giggled and pedaled away. "Tell me your name!"

Her answer floated on the wind. "Nora!"

BEN DECIDED to get a hotel room rather than drive all the way back to the Bay Area where he owned a small apartment. Seeing as Nora had effectively made him rearrange his schedule, he didn't see the point in making the three-hour drive when he was just going to turn right around in a few hours' time.

Nora was blind if she thought Emmett's Mill wasn't in a time warp. Driving through the sleepy town, he'd wondered how the place had managed to defy the touch of time. Everything was as he remembered as a kid, with the exception of the old Frosty. The ice-cream shop was gone and in its place was a razed spot with a sign that proclaimed the new offices of Grafton Realty were soon to come. His grandmother had taken him to the Frosty for vanilla soft-serve ice cream that summer he'd come to visit. His mouth twisted wryly. Visit—that's what his parents had called it. Ben had known, even at twelve, what it really was—an opportunity for Ben to get out of his parents' hair while they finalized their acrimonious divorce. As an adult he realized it had been a blessing; being at home while they tore each other to bits over every little detail would've been hell, but as a kid he'd just felt discarded.

Sighing, he moved away from his hotel window and went to the bed. An odd phantom sadness drifted over him when he thought of his grandparents. Aside from that one summer, he hadn't really known them. They sent cards on his birthday, but he had never been allowed to call. Their relationship with his father had soured for reasons unknown to him and he'd only been able to visit once. After he moved out and went to college, Ben managed to call a couple of times during odd moments of nostalgia but he hadn't really known what to say to them. They were nice but virtual strangers.

When he'd heard that they'd left the house to him instead of his father, he'd been stunned and his father had been pissed. His father's anger made no sense to him, but he'd long since stopped trying to decipher the man's mercurial moods. In fact, they rarely spoke. That was the advantage to living in separate states. His mother—Ben suppressed a weary groan—was another matter. Fortunately, for the moment she was too busy with the new love of her life to bother too much with Ben. He only hoped this one lasted. Penny Hollister-Ulacher-McDonald-Schlitz had a tendency to fall for the worst of men— his father included.

Without conscious thought, his mind drifted to Nora. He should've said something, revealed that he remembered her, but she'd taken him by surprise and he hadn't been prepared. Plus, the storm shooting from her gray eyes was alternately arousing and disconcerting. Her body had changed but her temperament certainly hadn't. He figured if she wasn't going to say anything, neither would he. It was probably easier this way, pretending neither knew the other. Kept the awkwardness—and the memories—at bay.

The last part wasn't quite true, but Ben had grown adept at ignoring even the most insistent inner voice. As a family law attorney for one of the most exclusive firms in the Bay Area, such talent was a requirement.

His BlackBerry chirped and he picked it up. His contemplative mood evaporated as he read a text message from the firm secretary, Celina, flashing on the small screen. He wasted no time in opening it, though his guts were roiling as he suspected what it would say.

Franklin says no go. You're on the Wallace case. Sorry.

Shit. Wallace versus Wallace. Classic case of love gone wrong with one kid as collateral damage. He tossed his BlackBerry to the bed and tried not to dwell, but this was one case he didn't want anything to do with. Ed Wallace was a despicable son of a bitch with loads of cash—and he wasn't willing to give one red cent of it to his wife despite her giving up her career to put him through college. Now she was in the same position many women found themselves in once their breadwinner husbands decided to trade them in for younger models. One with bigger, perkier boobs and a willingness to take a lot of crap for the perks that came with a loaded husband or boyfriend. And Franklin, the senior partner of Franklin, Mills & Donovan, wanted Ben on the case for reasons he was beginning to realize weren't something he'd want to announce at business meetings. *Ben Hollister, ruthless bastard. Nice to meet you.*

Ben shoved his hand through his hair. He couldn't stand to stay at Franklin, Mills & Donovan. He didn't want to enable one more scumbag to cheat his spouse out of her fair share just because he had more money than she did. Ben was beginning to feel soulless after each victory, as if he was destroying his humanity with each sweaty palm he shook in congratulations. But until he collected enough capital to open his own firm, he was stuck. Franklin, Mills & Donovan was the top of the food chain. When he made his move, it wouldn't be a step backward with a smaller or lesser firm; that's why he needed to open his own. His gaze drifted to the car parked outside his window. If it was his, he'd sell it in a heartbeat. Unfortunately it was simply on loan from his father, Dale. He allowed Ben to drive it when he was on the East Coast, which was where his father was most of the time, but the three or four times a year that he visited the West Coast, he liked to drive in style.

And although his mother was wealthy at the moment, thanks to Husband No. 4, Ben would rather crawl through raw sewage than ask her for money. Besides, even if he managed to swallow his pride and ask, there was no guarantee she'd give it. Her money was usually tied to the husband du jour, and the amount he'd need wouldn't go unnoticed. He sighed, scrubbing his hands across his face. His future, or more specifically, his sanity rested on selling his grandparents' house.

## CHAPTER TWO

"THESE AZALEAS are going to look lovely, Mrs. Pruitt," Nora exclaimed, leaning back to admire her own work as the elderly woman watched from her gardening chair while Nora did the actual planting. "I think the color really dresses up the yard, don't you think?"

"Oh, yes," Mrs. Pruitt breathed, a happy smile wreathing her aged face. Nora caught her expression falter ever so slightly as she added, "I just wish I was the one doing all the work. I do so miss my gardening. But you do a fantastic job for me."

"Well, thank you, Mrs. Pruitt. I take that as a high compliment coming from you. Now." She got up and dusted her knees, though the effort only removed some of the dirt ground into her worn jeans. "Let's take a look at that sprinkler system I set up for you. I've made it so easy, you don't even have to remember to turn it on. See this?

This is a timer that will do all the work for you."

"Bless your heart." Mrs. Pruitt's face wrinkled in a grin as they headed toward the house, her gait slow due to the walker. "You think of everything, don't you?"

"Well, not everything," she answered. Truthfully she should've installed the sprinkler the first time so the last batch of azaleas hadn't died. Mrs. Pruitt hadn't been able to get around as easily and the bright, colorful blooms had been one of the casualties. As if sensing her thoughts, Mrs. Pruitt's expression saddened.

"They were so beautiful. It plumb made me sick when I couldn't get to them. This old body just isn't the same anymore."

"Don't worry about it," Nora assured her, gesturing to the new plants. "Besides, I think that stock was weak. These ones are much hardier. I bought them from a new nursery."

She'd done no such thing, but the small fib was worth the relieved look Mrs. Pruitt gave her. "Well, if you say so, then I believe you," the elderly lady said, moving to the front door. "Are you coming in for some iced tea today?" she asked hopefully.

"Not today," she answered regretfully, noting the time. Nine o'clock—she was officially late. "I have another client. But I'll take a rain check, if that's all right with you."

Mrs. Pruitt nodded. "Of course, dear. I'll see you at the senior center, won't I?"

Nora made a show of looking scandalized. "Me? Miss Bingo? Surely you jest? Of course I'll be there. I'm determined to win that microwave or die shouting *Bingo* while trying."

Mrs. Pruitt tittered. "All right then, see you Wednesday."

Nora waited until Mrs. Pruitt disappeared into the house before clearing her garden space and packing away her tools. A quick glance at her clothes made her wonder if she should run home to change but on the heels of that thought she questioned why. It wasn't as if she were going out on a date. She was meeting a client—a coldhearted snake of a client with a deplorable memory but a client nonetheless. And since, basically, she worked with dirt in her chosen trade, it served to reason that she might have a bit of it on her clothes. And in her hair. How'd that get there? She shook her short hair free of the odd assortment of soil clumps that had somehow managed to station themselves there. She probably looked like Pigpen.

Good.

She hoped his aristocratic mouth pinched at the sight of her soiled and rumpled condition. It would probably go a long way toward quelling the ridiculous quiver that kept shivering her insides every time she thought of Ben Hollister.

She hauled her garden box into the back of her beat-up truck and headed out to the Hollister house. It was probably too much to ask for the man to have a paunchy belly and a balding pate, but it didn't stop her imagination from bloating the memory of a twelve-year-old Ben in a three-piece suit, trying to comb over the last remaining strands of his black hair. He was destined to lose his hair, she reasoned. B. J. Hollister had been as bald as Jean-Luc Picard, but he'd carried it nearly as well. She doubted Ben had the same poise—his character was much too weak.

Sliding from her seat, she paused long enough to lean over and grab her client notebook and then strode toward the house. She hadn't had time yesterday to truly note the house's flagging spirit, but now that she was in job mode it was hard not to see how quickly the old house had succumbed to the weather and vandals. The broken entry gate hung limply on its hinges by a single screw and looked as if a stiff wind would take it down. She had little time to bemoan the home's sad, victimized state as Ben suddenly appeared in the doorway and commanded her attention with his completely unbald and disgustingly fit state.

"You're late." His flat statement brooked no argument so she didn't try. Besides, there was no point in arguing fact—she was seven minutes late. His gaze swept her mussed appearance but he didn't comment. Disappointment washed over her as she realized she wanted him to disapprove. *Nora, you're gunning for a fight,* she chastised herself with a rueful grin. It wasn't like her to act childish but something about Ben brought out the worst in her. That didn't bode well for their working relationship.

"My other client ran long." She wanted to add that she was *only* seven minutes late, but judging by his stiff appearance, seven minutes might as well be an hour in his book. She mentally shrugged. Who cares? It wasn't as if they were dating. "Shall we begin?" she asked, pleased to hear her own voice resembling the professional she usually was under normal circumstances, even if she hadn't quite managed it thus far.

"Ah, right. So, as I told you yesterday, the place is a little run-down," he said, moving into the yard, kicking at the dead crabgrass with a disgusted motion that immediately set her blood percolating. Perhaps if he'd made more of an effort to see how his grandparents had been faring, the house might've been less derelict looking. "I talked with my Realtor yesterday after we spoke and she assured me a nice landscaping overhaul is sure to sweeten the offers, which at this point are nonexistent."

She ignored him and bent down to pull a dandelion from the ground, tossing it out of the yard and into the dirt driveway. The price was too high for the blue-collar residents of Emmett's Mill. Before B.J. and Corrinda bought the place, it had sat empty for close to ten years. And, although it was certainly a beautiful old home, it came with typical old-home problems. In other words, it was simply—as Ben called it—a money pit. But—she slid her gaze over to the sleek sports car and back to Ben—he looked as if he could afford what Nora wanted to do to this place. Honestly, she would've done it free of charge before the Hollisters died, but the old couple was proud and had waved away her offer every time. Now she could do something nice for them, even if it was under the guise of doing a job for their grandson.

She glanced up in time to see him tug at a lone, straggly rose, the petals floating to the ground to scatter in the slight breeze. "These'll be the first to go," he announced, and Nora looked at him sharply. He shrugged. "I hate roses."

"Why?"

"They're clichéd."

She blinked at his dismissive tone. "How is a flower clichéd?"

"It's not so much the flower but rather what they're used for."

"Enlighten me."

He crooked a cool grin, completely missing the sarcasm in her tone, and said, "Roses take little to no imagination on the part of the person sending them. What's the go-to flower for the new boyfriend? Long-stemmed roses. What's the first flower of choice for a husband who has cheated on his wife and is seeking to get back in her good graces? What's the flower of choice for heartbroken schmucks writing terrible poetry in the name of their loved ones? Roses. Red roses to be specific. And I'm not interested in seeing a bunch of rosebushes everywhere."

"Roses evoke a sense of culture and beauty that would complement this house," she said.

Something flitted across his face that almost qualified as pain, but it was gone before she had a chance to find out more, and in the next moment, he fixed her with a hard stare as he declared, "No roses."

Obviously he'd never seen a hybrid tea rose, such as the Gemini or the Condessa de Sastago, otherwise he would never make such an ignorant statement. She returned to her notes and bit her tongue in an attempt to keep her mouth from running away from her, but she was never good at keeping her mouth shut even when it was paramount.

"So if roses are so passé and clichéd, as you put it, what flowers would you send to your…girlfriend or significant other?"

"I don't send flowers."

"At all?"

"No."

"I bet the women cross crowded traffic to get to you," she snorted, suddenly feeling sorry for the women in his past who'd been suckered by his beautiful face only to find a heart of stone. "You sound like a *great* boyfriend. And when I say great, I mean crappy, in case you were confused."

Although she certainly hadn't meant the retort to be amusing, he reacted with a low and throaty chuckle that bordered on smug and made her want to smack him over the head with her clipboard.

"Haven't had any complaints yet," he said, sealing the coffin on her low opinion of him despite his looking like a Greek god masquerading as an Ivy-League-educated businessman. The man could benefit from being taken down a peg or two.

She graced him with a tight, completely saccharine smile. "That you know of. For all you know, your past lovers could be meeting once a month to compare your deficiencies—of which I'm sure there are many—over raspberry margaritas and tortilla chips." Her smile brightened at the thought. "You never know."

The superiority left his eyes, but his voice retained its infuriating confidence. "I doubt it but it's an entertaining thought."

Didn't the man recognize when he'd been slammed? She'd practically shot an arrow straight through an area most men were incredibly sensitive about, but he'd taken the hit as easily as if it had glanced off his shoulder. She'd have to try harder.

Back to business. "You know, Corrinda loved her roses," she said, unable to keep her thoughts on the subject completely professional. "She didn't seem to think they were clichéd at all. In fact, before her arthritis got really bad, her roses were some of the best. Everyone said so," she added for additional weight, though she wasn't sure why.

"Really?" His expression was contemplative as he reluctantly said, "I suppose it doesn't matter. It's not like I'll have to look at them every day. So you're saying the house will have a better chance at selling if we keep the rosebushes?"

Silently counting to ten, Nora continued, "I have no idea whether or not it would help the house sell. I just thought that you might want to keep them in deference to your *dead* grandmother." He gave her a blank look and she nearly bit her tongue in half.

*Insensitive lout.* Scratching out *American Beauty* from her notes, she gave him a terse, "Never mind" and moved on. "So, are there any other verboten flowers on your list?"

"Why does there need to be flowers at all?"

Oh, c'mon! "Because they're bright and pretty and always look nice when well tended." The man was a clod and had no sense of what makes a house a home.

"Your answer illustrates my point."

"Which is?"

"Who's going to tend them? My plans do

not include moving here to ensure the flowers stay pretty and bright, as you say. Likely, if the house doesn't sell right away they'll end up looking exactly as they do now."

"That's what automatic sprinkler systems are for," she countered, dismissing his comment. "Now—"

"Automatic anything sounds expensive. I was thinking of a rock or gravel garden with some cactus."

She made a face. "That sounds awful."

"Awful? Why?"

"Because it's a travesty to surround this gorgeous house with gravel and cacti. Besides, it would completely clash with the surroundings."

"But it would eliminate the need for constant care. I could hire a person to come out and weed now and then and it wouldn't run up a water bill."

Cheapskate. "Do you want the house to sell or not?"

His gaze narrowed. "That's a dumb question."

"Then let me do my job."

"I don't like your tone."

"What a coincidence. I don't like your attitude," she said, and they both stared at each other in hard-edged annoyance. Nora tucked her clipboard under her arm. "Listen, if you trust me, I'll do my best to make this house shine. I promise."

He looked ready to disagree or argue but didn't. Instead, he nodded grudgingly. Feeling she'd won the first of many battles, Nora kept her chortling to herself and focused on the next issue—money.

"I should tell you I require a ten-thousand-dollar deposit on jobs this extensive."

His eyes widened at the sum. "That seems a little high."

"That will cover any expenses and ensures that I get paid whether or not you change your mind."

"I'm not going to change my mind," he assured her.

Nora shrugged. "Doesn't matter. One bad experience has a way of making you gun shy. Ten-thousand—take it or leave it."

"Fine, but any other expenses that exceed that amount must be cleared by me before you proceed."

"Fair enough," she agreed. "Will that be personal check or credit card?"

"You'll take a check?"

She smiled. "As long as it's good."

"My checks are always good," he muttered

as he reached into his back pocket and pulled out a slim checkbook. *It must be nice to be able to write a check for that kind of money*, Nora thought abstractedly. She did well on her own but she wasn't a millionaire. Ben had the look of privilege and wealth, but B.J. and Corrinda had been practically broke when they died. In essence, the only thing of value had been the house, and even if the market had been favorable, they wouldn't have sold.

He handed her an executive draft and after she folded it in half, she stuck the check in her back pocket. "When will you start the work?" he asked.

"Soon. I'm going to take some soil samples, test the pH balance to see what I'm working with and then draw up some plans. When are you coming back into town so we can talk about the overall design?"

"Why don't you just fax them to my office—"

"No can do. No fax line. Besides, I prefer to do the walk-through in person." As much as she'd like to see less of Ben Hollister, she made a point never to start a job before explaining what she hoped to do with the property with the client. And she really didn't own a fax machine. She could probably find one but she wasn't interested in expending that kind of effort for him.

"Ms. Simmons, I'm sure you can appreciate how difficult it was for me to come up here. I'm an attorney with a full caseload. I can't just pop up here whenever you snap your fingers."

Laughter tickled her insides at the idea of Ben popping anywhere but she prickled at the implication that his time was more valuable than hers. "Why do you want to open your own firm if you're already so busy?" she asked, noting quickly how his demeanor changed at the innocent question. Sore spot. Good to know. "What kind of law do you practice? Corporate? Personal injury? Or something completely dry and boring like contract law?"

His mouth tightened and he all but gritted his teeth when he answered. "Family law. Divorces, mainly."

How perfect. Nora imagined Ben was a shark in court. She could sense a ruthlessness in him that made goose bumps riot across her exposed skin in what should've been a warning sign, but Nora never ran from a challenge.

"Family law? So you went into the family business, huh?"

Ben stiffened and his eyes became wary and she wondered if the attitude came with the law degree or if it was something he came by naturally.

"Normally I don't like lawyers, but B.J. managed to bend my opinion a little. He always had lollipops for the little kids who came into his office and a joke up his sleeve." She slid her gaze to Ben. "Are you sure you're related?"

It came out as a joke, but a part of her wasn't kidding. It didn't seem natural that Ben, a man who would be the last person to offer a kid a sucker for fear of a choking liability, would share genes with someone as gentle and funny as B. J. Hollister.

Ben ignored her question. "I'll see what I can do with my schedule. I might be able to squeeze out one day next week."

"Great."

"Anything else?"

*Tell me why you never came back.* "Nope. That's it."

"Good. I'll leave you to come back to me with a plan and we'll go from there. Remember, we agreed no roses."

*We didn't agree. I got frustrated and dropped the subject,* she wanted to yell but didn't.

She tapped her head. "It's all up here. Don't worry, I won't steer you wrong."

"I know."

For a split second she thought she saw truth reflected through his gaze, as if he trusted her despite her sharp tongue and blatant attempts to goad him, and the fleeting glimpse left her off-kilter.

"All right then," she said, moving slowly toward the front gate, a bit concerned by her sudden desire to stick around. They weren't friends. They weren't anything but client and employee. "I'll be in touch." She started for the gate then doubled back, realizing she ought to give him a business card this time.

"Thank you." He accepted the card and their fingers brushed. The contact was minute, but it was enough to send an electric zap down the length of her arm and end with little pops and gasps at the pit of her stomach. She yanked her hand back and the corner of his mouth lifted in subtle acknowledgment. She eyed him suspiciously. Had he felt it, too?

But he offered nothing, saying, "I look forward to hearing your ideas," before ascending the front steps and disappearing into the house.

Nora's mouth dried conspicuously and she stared down at her offending fingers, all too aware of the physical reaction to Ben's brief touch. Grimacing, she wiped her hand on the back of her jeans and stalked to her truck. She'd never been the type to act all fluttery and girlie over a guy. Wasn't her style. She would much rather hang out with the guys than the girls any day.

She was a tomboy in a woman's body. Nora glowered at the house, more specifically at Ben inside, and jerked the truck into gear. Not gonna happen.

## CHAPTER THREE

BEN LET THE DOOR close behind him and listened as Nora's truck rumbled down the weed-choked driveway to the highway until the sound faded to nothing.

The card in his hand still felt warm, as if it had sat in the sun all day, and he could almost imagine the heat was from Nora herself.

There was something about her that drew him without conscious thought. Something unguarded and free. The same quality she'd exuded as a kid. Life might've leached it out of someone else but not Nora. He wondered how some people managed to hold on to that quality yet others lost it. Stepping from the foyer into the expansive hallway that dissected the house into separate rooms, he drew a deep breath and pushed Nora out of his mind.

The house was utterly still; the walls were covered with antique clocks, mostly of the cuckoo variety, but without someone to reset their chains, they hung silent. Ben remembered the constant ticktock—and cuckoos—from his summer visit years ago, and how he had found the noise distracting the first night. But by the end of the week, the odd cacophony was soothing and he'd slept like a baby.

In the absence of such sounds, the silence was unnatural.

He wandered to the nearest Black Forest clock, enticed by old memories, and gently pulled the pine weights, the mechanism inside moving smoothly despite its age, and then he pushed the tiny hands into their proper place. Finally, he gave the small pendulum bob a light tap to set it swinging.

The soft, distinct ticking replaced the disquieting stillness and he inhaled against the tight feeling in his chest. He hadn't known the man long, but he remembered how much his grandfather had loved these clocks. A slow turn around the room revealed countless in pristine shape. Every available wall was crammed with them. Ben leaned in to take a better look at the clock he'd just reset and even though he wasn't an expert, he could guess they were worth something to the right person.

And the house was filled with them.

He could sell the clocks at auction. As quickly as the thought came, he discarded it. He didn't know what to do with them, but the thought of selling them left him cold. But Ben couldn't very well tote around hundreds of clocks. It wasn't practical. Selling most of them was probably what he'd end up doing.

Moving through the first floor, he took careful note of the worn spots in the faded sofa set where sunlight had bleached the once-vibrant fabric and shone through moth-eaten areas in the drapes over the cobwebbed bay window. The wood floor was dull and scratched in many places and would need a complete overhaul if he wanted to use it as a selling point.

A shadow of regret settled on his thoughts as he looked around the house. After that one summer, his father had refused to allow him to return, and as the years went by, the desire to visit faded. Now, standing in his grandparents' home, surrounded by their possessions, he realized he should've made more of an effort. He could've helped out monetarily if nothing else. Judging by the house's appearance, it seemed they'd had little to spare. That in itself puzzled him more than he wanted to admit. His grandfather had been an attorney here—surely there were enough clients, even in a town as small as Emmett's Mill, to support one little old couple? Without saying it aloud, he resolved to ask around if he found time.

He grimaced. The repairs were bound to be expensive. He'd have to tap his trust, though it wasn't something he wanted to do. He didn't have millions, just a little over one hundred grand. He'd have to be careful— home repairs, especially on places this old, could get ridiculous.

Ben made a cursory tour of the rest of the house and found it in similar condition.

Moving to the large window that looked out behind the house and down the hill, he saw the winding creek below, the water shimmering in the light, catching the sun rays and tossing them back in a glorious dance of sunshine and sky.

He glanced down at his shoes. Brown dress loafers stared back at him. Not the least bit appropriate for going hiking. There used to be a path from the house to Nora's favorite swimming hole, the one where he'd first found her that summer. He wondered if anyone went there anymore. The path was probably overgrown by now.

Dismissing the idea before it had the chance to germinate, he walked away from the window.

He didn't have time to wind clocks or think about traipsing around the creek where he'd no doubt trudge right through poison oak because, as Nora so aptly put at the tender age of ten, he was no country boy. A sound of annoyance escaped him as he left the house and he quickly locked up. He had to get back to the city. Back to his life.

"YOU'RE UNUSUALLY QUIET tonight," Natalie observed later that night while at their father's for dinner. Since their mom died last year of pancreatic cancer, Natalie made it her job to ensure their dad was okay, as if the man were going to slowly die of starvation. Nora looked up from her plate and realized she'd been staring at her carrots, her thoughts stuck in a direction they shouldn't be. Natalie's comment drew Tasha's attention and now both her older sisters were staring at her, their husbands joining them seconds later. "Is everything okay?"

She squirmed under everyone's gaze. "Everything's fine," Nora told Natalie, but it wasn't entirely true. She was replaying her earlier meeting with Ben in her head, looking for some clue that he hadn't really forgotten her. Of course, she had the misfortune to remember every single nuance of their acquaintance because it wasn't every day a girl got her first kiss. She could admit it, her ego was bruised. She'd just come to the conclusion that Ben had to have remembered her, when Natalie drew her attention again.

"Janelle came into the bookstore a few weeks ago and mentioned that the Hollister house is on the market and has been for the past four months," Natalie said, making conversation. "I think she was dropping a hint that Evan and I ought to look into buying it but I told her we were happy with our little place. I wonder who will buy it."

Gerald Simmons appeared mildly interested at the subject change. "Don't imagine it's going to sell anytime soon."

Nora agreed with her dad.

Natalie placed her wiggling one-year-old son, Justin Cole, into her husband's arms so she could help their three-year-old, Colton Jeremiah, with his hamburger. "It's a beautiful house, but I don't know who could afford it. I didn't tell Janelle that, though. I didn't want to seem pessimistic."

"Before the Hollisters bought it, it sat empty for years. There was talk of donating it to the historical society, but no one had the money to relocate it into town, so the owners just let it sit. Damn shame," Gerald said, excusing himself from the table. Natalie rose to see if he needed anything but he waved her away.

"Will you stop mothering him, for crying out loud?" Nora muttered in annoyance. "He's fine. You're driving him crazy."

"I am not," Natalie retorted indignantly. "He's still not recovered from Mom's death. I worry about him."

Tasha intervened, motioning to Nora. "Down, girl. I think Natalie's right, though. Something's got you all preoccupied. Care to share?"

Nora thought about it, then answered, "No, not really."

"Oh, I see how it is. You get to pry into our business, but when it comes to yours, it's off-limits?" Tasha teased.

"You're a smart woman," Nora said, sparing a glance at her sister.

Natalie's husband, Evan, and Tasha's husband, Josh, took that as a cue to leave the women to their discussion and Nora was half tempted to follow their lead. She didn't feel ready to discuss Ben. *Why not?* a voice demanded, her inner psyche realizing Nora was squirming. It wasn't as if he meant anything to her. So they'd kissed years ago. Big deal. If Nora lined up all the men she'd kissed in her lifetime, they'd probably reach from here to Coldwater. Well, that was exaggerating, but there were a few. And none of them made her think twice or dwell on it.

Natalie recovered from Nora's earlier remark to ask, "Didn't you know the Hollisters?"

"Yes. They were the cutest couple. Totally in love even after fifty-some odd years of marriage. I met them at the senior center at a bingo night." She glanced at her sister. "Why?"

"The name rang a bell. I seem to remember one summer when a certain boy…Ben, I believe his name was…"

Natalie was baiting her and it was working. Nora looked away. Tasha leaned in, interest etched on her face, while Natalie continued with a playful gleam in her eye.

"When Nora was little…she used to go swimming in the creek behind that big house, even though she wasn't supposed to ride her bike that far down the road."

"Such a rebel," Tasha said, clucking her tongue like an old lady.

Nora snorted. "I wasn't the one to run off and join the Peace Corps. I believe that was you. We've got the postcards to prove it."

"Touché," Tasha said, but her green eyes danced with mirth at how Nora was obviously trying to deflect the conversation.

Natalie continued, enjoying herself. "And, I remember a certain someone coming home one day looking like she'd just gotten her first taste of chocolate cheesecake with an extra dollop of fresh whipped cream."

"Are you pregnant again?" Nora asked. "Last time you started to use food analogies you were knocked up."

"I'm not pregnant," Natalie assured her, sending a conspiratorial look Tasha's way. "The question is, did you kiss the Hollisters' grandson, little sister?"

Tasha broke out in a peal of laughter when Nora's cheeks reddened in answer, and Natalie nearly jumped out of her chair in victory. "I knew it! I always wondered but never asked. How old were you? Nine? Ten?"

"Ten," Nora grumbled, wishing she'd left the room when she'd had the chance. She speared Tasha with a dirty look. "It's all your fault, you know."

Tasha sobered with difficulty. "How is it my fault?" she choked out.

"If I hadn't seen you kissing Josh all the time I wouldn't have been so curious. I wanted to know what all the fuss was about."

Tasha and Josh had been high-school sweethearts, and like most teenagers, whenever they thought they were alone, they couldn't keep their hands off each other.

"You were watching? You little perv," Tasha said, grinning.

"Well, what do you expect? It was kind of hard to miss. You guys kept stealing all my good hiding places."

Tasha's eyes turned misty as she reminisced, then as her husband walked by, the look turned primal.

"Ugh, it's my childhood all over again. Get a room." Nora grabbed her plate and walked to the adjoining kitchen.

Sisters, she grumbled to the sink as she rinsed her plate, were a pain in the ass because they saw way too much when you didn't want to share. But, even as she shied away from sharing her recent experience with Ben, a part of her needed their perspective. Sighing, she returned to the dining room.

"Here's the deal," Nora said, ignoring their knowing expressions. "The Hollisters left the house to their grandson, Ben, who has now hired me to overhaul the outside landscaping so that he can sell it."

"Why does he want to sell?" Natalie asked.

"He wants to open his own law practice in

the Bay Area. Noble cause, I know. Personally, I think it's pretty cold but it doesn't
matter. I think he'll have trouble selling it."

"Why?" Tasha returned, puzzled. "After
you're finished with the place, it'll look like
a *Better Homes and Gardens* special."

"It's too expensive," both Nora and Natalie
said in unison.

"Like Dad said, that house sat for years
before the Hollisters bought it," Nora added.
"It's too much house for the older, retired set
who might be able to afford it and way too expensive for the young families who might
actually put it to good use. Plus, it's on the
outskirts of town and when it snows, the
driveway virtually disappears. Since it's
private property it doesn't get plowed by the
county."

"Did you tell Ben this?" Tasha asked.

She turned to Tasha. "No. And I don't plan
to."

"Why not?" Tasha's expression turned
speculative. "Seems like pertinent information for your client."

Nora lifted her chin. "I don't care. He
doesn't deserve to know."

Natalie looked puzzled, then concerned.
"I don't understand. Why doesn't he
deserve to know?"

"Do you realize he only visited his grand-parents once in his lifetime? What kind of person is that? Frankly, I don't want to reward that kind of behavior."

"You're not his mother, you're his employee. I think you're making a mistake," Natalie said.

"Maybe I'll buy it," Nora said, although the idea had only just popped into her head. "I've always liked the house and I'll take care of it far better than Ben."

"Can you afford it?" Tasha asked tentatively and Nora shifted in her chair under her scrutiny.

"Umm…well, not yet but maybe by the time I finish the job." And a few others, she thought with a private wince.

"Nora…" Natalie's tone had a warning to it that Nora hated. She always had a way of making Nora feel like the baby even though she was thirty-two. "What are you doing? I've never seen you act like this… Well, I take that back, there was one other time…"

Nora stiffened, knowing exactly what time Natalie was referring to and she shot her a dark look. "It's nothing like that."

"Like what?" Tasha asked. "I hate being out of the loop. What happened before?"

"Thanks a lot, Nat. You know, you don't

like everyone to know you got pregnant from a one-night stand with your river guide, maybe I don't like everyone to know I slept with a client who turned out to be married."

"I married my river guide, thank you very much," Natalie retorted. "And don't get on your high horse. When it comes to secrets it isn't like you're the locked box. You can't wait to butt your nose into everyone's business." She turned to Tasha. "Why do you think she hangs out with all those seniors? They love to gossip as much as she does."

"I hang out with them because they're good people and they're far more interesting than everyone else. You included these days."

"Little sister, you've got juicy secrets," Tasha teased, plainly happy to be included even if Nora's mood was bordering dangerously on annoyed. "A married man. Details, please."

"No." Nora got up and walked back into the kitchen to grab a beer from the fridge, but it was empty. She leaned out and hollered to Natalie because she was in charge of the groceries for Dad. "Where's the Bud Light?"

"Dad doesn't need that stuff. I stopped buying it," Natalie hollered back.

She ground her teeth and made a note to buy some for Dad tomorrow. The man lost his wife, the least Natalie could do is let him have his beer.

She returned to see Tasha and Natalie in a hushed conversation that they immediately stopped the moment she reentered the room. Nora wasn't stupid; they were talking about Griffin. A girl couldn't make a mistake without having it broadcasted in this family. She glared at Natalie. "He didn't tell me he was married and he never wore a ring. How was I supposed to know?"

Griffin was a subject she hated to visit. It served to remind her why she didn't let people get under her skin. She'd fallen hard and he'd let her fall face-first in a big pile of humiliation. The scene with the wife had been particularly mortifying.

Tasha sensed Nora withdraw and changed the subject, or rather returned to their original discussion—not that Nora was relieved. She didn't want to talk about that, either. Frankly, she was ready to go home. In her present frame of mind, it'd been a mistake to come tonight, but Natalie was adamant they come to these dinners for Dad. Nora liked to say she went so Natalie would stop hounding but she enjoyed seeing her nephews. They were the cutest little suckers and Nora couldn't get enough of them.

"So tell me again why you can't stand this guy?"

Nora considered her answer, looking for the most succinct way to convey her feelings when they were in a tumbled mess inside her head. "The Hollisters were good people and they adored him. Always talked about how much they hoped he'd come to visit when he was older. They were so proud of him for going to Harvard Law and becoming an attorney. But he couldn't come to visit a handful of times to make his grandparents feel loved instead of forgotten?" she said, making what she thought was a serious point in her favor until Natalie fixed her with a "big sister" look that she'd perfected while Tasha was away at college and then the Peace Corps. Nora sighed. Sometimes she didn't even know why she opened her mouth.

"Do you want my opinion?" Natalie asked.

"No."

"Too bad. I think you should find someone else to do the job. It's obvious you're not acting in the best interests of your client."

Nora glowered at Natalie. Why did she have to be such a Dudley Do-Right? Would it kill her to just go with the moment?

"There's no rule that says I have to like someone I work for. I'll do the job, collect the cash and be gone."

"If it's that simple, why are you acting like something's bit you in the ass tonight?" Natalie asked. "I think it bothers you that you have feelings of some sort for this guy and you're doing everything you can to fight them."

"That's ridiculous," Nora said, but her cheeks flared. "This isn't the fourth grade, Natalie. Besides, if you met the guy you'd agree with me that he's an arrogant jerk." With an amazing set of eyes and a physique that could make a nun sit up and take notice. "A class-A jerk with an Ivy-League pedigree. *So* not my type."

Natalie offered a smug smile and Nora wanted to groan, but Tasha distracted her.

"Nat is right. I think you should pull out. There's no way you can be objective here and whether you realize it or not, you're sabotaging your client with your animosity. You need to think rationally, not emotionally in this situation. This involves your career. Besides, you're better than that."

"Who says?"

"We do," her sisters answered in unison.

"Oh, kiss my butt," Nora grumbled, but she was wavering. If the job were for anyone else, she wouldn't care. But it was Ben. The truth of the matter was, she'd harbored a secret crush for years after that one kiss. She'd spent each summer hoping he'd come back but he hadn't. After each disappointment, her crush had turned to resentment. It was irrational, which was why she'd never shared her feelings with her sisters, but it didn't change the way she felt.

"B.J. and Corrinda were good people. They deserve better than what their grandson gave them," she said stubbornly, ignoring her sisters' advice. "I'm doing this for them."

"Well, that might be true, but just be careful about judging others when you don't know their circumstances," Tasha said. "It could change your perspective. What did Ben say when he realized it was you?"

Her cheeks heated. "Nothing. He didn't remember."

Natalie's eyes widened but there was laughter in them. "He didn't remember you? That's hard to believe. Your personality is…well, either people like you or hate you. There's no gray area."

Nora agreed but didn't feel the need to say so. She shrugged. "He didn't say anything so I didn't, either. No point in rubbing it in my face that I'm nothing in his memory." *When for years I used to replay that one brief moment over and over in my mind, making it bigger and more wonderful in my head with each passing day.* What an idiot. "Besides, it's better this way. It's not like either one of us is hoping for a reunion tour. I can't stand him and I think the feeling is mutual."

"So why'd he hire you?" Natalie asked.

"Because I'm the best."

Natalie sighed. "At least he's not dumb."

Tasha's speculative look had Nora staring at her in suspicion. "What?"

"What if he does remember you and just isn't saying anything?" Tasha wondered aloud.

"You know, for a second I wondered that, too. I thought it seemed a little weird, but if on the off chance he was being genuine, I wasn't about to embarrass myself," Nora said.

Tasha laughed. "Maybe he thought saying something might make things awkward between you. He probably didn't want there to be any kind of barrier between you as employer and client. Makes sense to me, especially if neither of you is interested in reliving the past."

"Whatever." Nora tapped her fingers against the tabletop in a rapid, agitated movement. Damn. Tasha's theory made sense to her, too, but that made it worse. If he really remembered her, he should've said something. Somehow his omission seemed fraudulent. "I'll tell him tomorrow," she said glumly, hating that her sisters had talked her out of avenging her childish disappointment. She must be getting old.

BEN KEPT HIS PEN still while Ed Wallace, as pompous as he was self-centered, rejected the latest offer presented by his soon-to-be ex-wife's camp.

"Forget it. If I agree to that I'll be paying her for the rest of my life, plus I'll have to sell my new yacht to meet the settlement."

Ben drew a measured breath while his patience for the man fluctuated between barely there and nonexistent. "It's not a bad offer. Probably better than you'll get if we go to court. You're paying me for my counsel. Take the deal."

"I'm paying you to get me out of giving my ex-wife everything I've worked for for the past twenty years to achieve," Ed growled. "Or have you forgotten that?"

Ben met the man's hard stare with one of his own. Ginny Wallace was being much more lenient than she could afford to be in

Ben's opinion, but Ed couldn't see past his own greed to take the offer before she came to her senses. "You're worth ten million today. Twenty years ago, when you were a busboy at some small restaurant in Oakland and met a young waitress named Ginny, you were worth zip. You probably had twenty dollars in your pocket on payday. She quit college so you could get your business degree and later your master's. If we go to court, you'll lose. And that yacht will be the first thing to go."

"She's no saint," Ed retorted, his gaze darting away from Ben.

"No, but if this goes to court, she's got a pretty good case. Even in a no-fault state like California, judges tend to turn a jaundiced eye toward men who look like they're just trading up when the old model no longer shines. Let's face it, Ed, you've been seen all around town with a busty blonde half your age. You and I know the only reason she's on your arm is your money. If you go to court, you'll have a whole lot less of it."

Ed's face turned an ugly shade of red and he shifted in his chair before adjusting his tie with slow, deliberate movements. "It's a good thing I have you then, isn't it? I know you got Harold Crimshaw off and his ex-wife was a cripple. Last I heard she was living on disability with a small supplement from her settlement. How much did she end up with? Barely fifty thousand from what I remember…" His expression turned mildly generous, though on his hard facial planes it still held an edge of malice. "I'm not asking for a miracle. Just something fair. I don't want to pay more than one million. Not a penny more. Got it?"

Ben withheld his snarl. The man deserved no less than a kick to the groin. He was half tempted to sabotage the case and offer some pointers to the other side. The image of Sherry Crimshaw's stricken face was with him every time he walked into a courtroom with another scumbag millionaire looking to get off scot-free after discarding the wives that stood behind them when they had nothing.

Ed was right. Ben had enabled Harold to bilk his wife out of her rightful share by twisting the facts. Harold had claimed Sherry was an alcoholic and the accident that put her into a wheelchair had been her fault. With Harold's help, Ben managed to convince the judge that Harold was the poor husband who could no longer allow his drunken wife to drag him down. A piece of Ben's humanity broke off that day.

The worst part? The look of pride on his father's face. He'd flown in just to watch Ben in action. It was that much more awful because for years he'd yearned for that look and never received it; but the day he had, the reasons made him ill. He didn't want to be like his father and the fact that he seemed to have inherited his father's skill for decimating innocent witnesses wasn't something Ben wanted to crow about.

Now, each case too close in circumstance to Sherry's made him realize how much of a bastard he was to help these people. He wasn't kidding himself; he wasn't a saint, either. Ben had no visions of opening a free clinic, but he wanted the choice to decline a client. Right now, he was at the beck and call of the firm. And the firm catered to assholes like Ed Wallace and Harold Crimshaw.

It was moments like this that made him wonder how he ended up in a place like Franklin, Mills & Donovan.

## CHAPTER FOUR

NORA SAT on her front porch with her best friend, Sammy Halvorsen, sharing a beer and watching the sun sink in the horizon. She tried to derail her annoying train of thought, but wasn't doing such a bang-up job. Despite her attempts to enjoy Sammy's company and the visual pleasure of a brilliant burnt-orange sunset, she couldn't stop thinking—no, obsessing—on one thing.

She turned to Sammy. "Can I ask you something?"

Sammy paused, Corona bottle halfway to his lips, at Nora's pensive question. "Sure."

The call of a red-shouldered hawk split the air from atop the forested skyline and echoed against Bald Rock. Nora waited until the sound faded, replaced by the crickets' night song. "Do guys forget their first kiss?"

Sammy lifted the bottle to his mouth. "Nope."

"I didn't think so," she said. "I'd be

willing to bet my right foot he remembers perfectly clear."

"Who remembers?"

"Ben Hollister."

"Who's that? I don't recall the name from school. He a client or something?"

"Sort of."

Sammy reached for a fresh Corona from his small cooler and cracked it. "We gonna play Twenty Questions or are you going to start making sense?"

Nora drew a deep breath, but her mouth retained its tightness.

"You okay?"

"It's stupid," she admitted. "I can't believe I'm even letting my brain think about it, but for some reason I can't let it go and it's driving me crazy." She swigged her own beer before continuing, needing the alcohol to give her courage. If it were anyone but Sammy sitting beside her she wouldn't divulge anything, but she trusted him with her secrets and he'd never let her down. Plus, he had the right chromosomal makeup to answer her question. She might feel comfortable acting like a guy in many ways, but her brain was still decidedly female. "He's pretending not to remember me. I find that hard to believe. Who was the first girl you ever kissed?"

"Connie Villiandi," he answered without hesitation. "Mmm. All puckered lips and strawberry-flavored lip gloss."

"Connie?" Nora repeated, distracted by his revelation and his lazy grin. She snorted in something akin to disgust and his cheeks flared with heat. "The girl couldn't catch a pitch to save her life and acted like the prom queen at twelve. Geez, Sammy, my respect level for you just took a nosedive."

"Yeah, well, that girl turned into a very smart woman. Last I heard, she was working some government job with top-secret clearance. Not everyone is a jock like you, Nora."

"You're right. I'm sorry. I'm all jacked up because of this thing with Ben."

"Which is?"

Nora sighed and shook her head. Curiosity thoroughly pricked, he gestured impatiently for her to get on with it.

"I'm not getting any younger, Simmons. Out with it. Wait…is this something I'm going to feel obligated to kick this guy's ass over?"

She chuckled in amusement. "I've got a meaner left hook than you."

Sammy worked his jaw in memory. "You got that right. So what is it?"

"Ben Hollister is my new client. His

grandparents owned the big Victorian just outside of town."

"Are they that old couple who died in that bad accident on Highway 41?"

"Yes, and they left the house to their only grandson. He's hired me to fix up the landscaping so the house will sell. The thing is…I've met him before."

Sammy gave her a blank stare. "Yeah, so?"

"He came to Emmett's Mill one summer when we were kids and, well, we kissed."

He grinned. "Was it weird between you?"

She looked at him sharply. "When?"

He gestured. "Today, now, whenever you saw him again."

Her shoulders relinquished some of their stiffness but her jaw still felt tense. She blew a hard breath and shrugged. "Yes, I mean no. He didn't seem to remember me and I didn't know how to bring it up without looking like a complete idiot. What was I supposed to say? 'Hey, good to see you, Ben. You've sure changed a lot from the boy I kissed down at the swimming hole.'"

"You could start there but I'd finesse it a little more," Sammy offered before breaking into a wide smile. "How old were you?"

"Ten."

"Ten! I can't believe you beat me to it!

And to a kid who was just passing through. Un-freaking-believable."

"Oh, get over it. Stay on topic, please. So now my sisters are saying that I should just come out and tell him, because it wasn't right for me to go on pretending that we're strangers, but why should I when he seems perfectly content to go on pretending?"

"From a guy's standpoint, I'd say he didn't want to be embarrassed if you didn't remember him. It goes both ways, you know."

Nora made a sound of disbelief and rose to grab another Corona from Sammy's cooler. She returned to the old rocker and propped her feet on the porch railing, rocking the chair as she lifted the bottle to her lips. "So you're saying that it's possible he didn't say anything because *he* was afraid I might not remember him?"

"What can I say? We men have fragile egos."

"Not this guy," she mumbled, leaning down to place her beer on the weathered wooden planks of the porch. "He's got confidence oozing out his pores like cheap cologne. It's called eau de conceit. Somehow I doubt he's sitting at home wondering if I remember him." She barked a laugh. "The thought is ludicrous."

"So just ask him."

"Like it's that simple."

"Uh…it is. Open your mouth and just ask. You've never seemed to have a problem with asking anyone anything in the past. I still remember Rocky Slonik's expression when you asked him point-blank why one of his ears was bigger than the other. Poor kid blushed five different shades of red you embarrassed him so bad."

Nora grimaced, picturing that long-ago scene only too well. "Yeah, I'm an expert at shoving my foot in my mouth. Sometimes I wish I were more like Natalie. She's always doing the right thing. Even Tasha knows when to shut the hell up and take the high road. Maybe I'm the defective sister."

"Maybe."

She grinned. "You're an asshole."

He lifted his beer in thanks. "Card-carrying member from what I've heard."

"That's probably why we've been friends for so long. We're both defective. Peas in a messed-up pod. Aren't we the lucky ones?"

"Amen, sistah."

Nora laughed and retrieved her beer. "So who you seeing this week?" she asked, her heart much lighter than earlier in the evening. It was hard to stay in a bad mood with Sammy around, the guy's sense of humor was infectious. She shot him a curious look when he failed to answer right away.

"Holding out on me, Halvorsen?"

He grinned but his eyes didn't follow. Nora sat straighter. "Now it's my turn, I see. What's going on?"

"Nothing. Just been a long day."

"Tell me about it. I got nothing but the rest of the night to burn and we've got a few more Coronas to kill. I'm all ears, pretty boy."

He shrugged, the motion nonchalant enough, but he began playing with his beer bottle, focusing on his hands rather than the conversation. Nora should've seen something was eating at him when he showed up with beer but she'd been too concerned with what was going on in her own head. Some best friend she was. She made a point to try harder. "C'mon, am I going to have to play Twenty Questions or what?" she teased, using his own words against him.

He smiled but it was followed by a difficult sigh. "I think I'm getting old. I've been worried about things that never bothered me before."

"Such as?"

"I started thinking about where I'm going

KIMBERLY VAN METER                81

to be in a few years and I didn't like what I saw."

"What are you talking about? You've got it made. You work with your brothers in a successful family business, you make decent money and you're not in debt. What's the problem?"

"Nothing, I guess."

Unconvinced by his tone, she pressed harder. If there was one thing she excelled at, it was getting information out of someone. "Sam, what's eating at you?"

His gaze left his beer bottle and traveled out toward the darkening sky. The automatic porch light switched on, followed by the bug lamp. Soon the air would be filled with the sound of insects meeting their doom in one loud electric zap. She considered moving their powwow inside, but didn't want to disrupt what he was working up to share. The decision turned out to be wise, for Sammy turned to her a moment later, his hazel eyes troubled. "I'm just starting to wonder if I'm looking for love in all the wrong places."

"I didn't know you were looking for love at all." For as long as Sammy had been noticing the opposite sex, he'd never been one for commitment. He was a genuine player in the field of serial dating.

"Yeah, me neither," he admitted. "I guess I figured I'm not a kid anymore. The idea of being alone doesn't sound very appealing."

"So don't be alone," she suggested. "You're never at a loss for finding willing and eager women to share your time."

He nodded but Nora got the impression she'd hadn't been much help. Something turbulent remained trapped behind his eyes, but he didn't give her a chance to try again.

"Thanks for the company, but I gotta get going." He rose from the battered wicker chair and scooped up his six-pack Igloo cooler. "Dean's got a big job for us tomorrow and he ain't big on sympathy when you're dragging your butt 'cause you stayed up too late."

"Gotta love older brothers."

"Yeah. Something like that."

He headed down the stairs until her voice stopped him.

"Sammy, if you need to talk I'm here."

He lifted his cooler in acknowledgment. "Thanks."

THE SPORTS CAR PURRED along the country back road, eating up the miles between the bay and Emmett's Mill as the sun crested the east, slanting bright yellow morning sun through Ben's window. The brisk California air reminded him that it was too early to take the top down, but Ben had wanted to feel something other than the damp fog of the bay. The sunshine, though not exactly warm yet, was a welcome change.

He and Nora were meeting today to discuss her plans for the landscaping and that's all he wanted to think about.

He didn't want to consider this an escape, but there was no mistaking that he was humming and actually smiling.

A change of scenery was always good.

His good mood didn't have anything to do with Nora.

He geared down to take a sharp turn; the high-performance vehicle responded with a low, throaty growl as he accelerated out of the turn. If nothing else, the ride was enjoyable.

Miles of road stretched ahead of him and he relaxed. Before long a memory floated out of his mental lockbox and startled him with the feelings it aroused.

The kiss.

A brief smile ghosted his lips.

It was so easy to see the scene in his mind, hear the water gurgling over stone slabs and smell the faint odor of algae and moss that collected in the areas where the water didn't run freely. He could also smell the coconut suntan lotion on her golden skin, see the white-gold of her hair spilling in a wild nest around her shoulders.

"It's really an experiment," she'd said primly one day. "I need to see what all the fuss is about when it comes to this kissing stuff. Tasha does it *every time* she sees her boyfriend, Josh, and I want to see why she likes to do it."

"Why don't you just ask her?" he suggested, not entirely sure he should be kissing a ten-year-old. But she was kind of cute and persistent and, honestly, he was curious to see if she would truly go through with it.

Nora's young face screwed into a scowl. "She says I'm too young to understand, but I'm not. I'm the smartest in my class and I want to know. Are you going to help me out or what?"

He took a moment to think about it. Truth was, he'd never kissed anyone either.

She put her hands on her hips. "Well?"

"Well…I guess. What do you want to do?"

Nora came to him with a stern expression. "You have to put your arms around me like this," she instructed, nodding in approval once Ben's arms closed around her small frame. "Okay, now I'll put my arms around your waist and then you'll bend down and I'll reach on my tippy-toes and we'll meet in the middle with our lips. Got it?"

"Sounds simple enough," he said, hoping no one happened to walk by this particular stretch of creek when he placed a soft kiss on her baby lips, catching the lingering scent of bubble gum on her breath. He pulled away. Her eyelids were closed and he could've sworn he felt her heart racing. Faint blue veins ran a course over her lids and her cheeks had pinked despite her golden summer tan. She was probably the prettiest girl he'd ever seen. Her eyes popped open and in a surprising motion, she jerked away with a halting nod.

"Experiment concluded! Bye!"

And then she was gone.

He'd hoped to catch her around town, but even as small as Emmett's Mill was, they hadn't managed to bump into each other again. A few days later he returned to New England, his life unrecognizable from what it'd been.

The enjoyable feelings of that long-ago kiss faded with what followed that summer. He hated that this particular memory still had the power to make him feel small and vulnerable.

Ben breathed deep the clean air and pushed away the dark feelings crawling around in his chest. Divorce was a fact of life. This was something he dealt with every day. Irreconcilable differences. He read that on the paperwork that came across his desk so many times, he once spent some idle time trying to figure out how to spell it phonetically on a personalized license plate for his car. As a family law attorney who specialized in ugly divorces, he thought the idea was darkly tongue-in-cheek. His girlfriend at the time hadn't agreed. As he recalled, she'd said that such a cynical view was pessimistic about love in general. That's when he'd blithely dropped the bomb—he didn't believe in love. She wasn't around anymore.

He'd yet to meet someone who wasn't hung up on the idea of true love and all that crap. Personally he was sick of playing the game. The next woman he invited into his life would be one who shared the same sentiment toward love. He didn't have the time to deal with someone who was looking for their soul mate.

What about someone who commands kisses in the name of science…?

No time for that either, but he had to admit, the thought was intriguing.

# CHAPTER FIVE

"ARE YOU *ever* on time?"

Nora strode toward Ben and ignored his tone. Despite the stuffiness of his earthy-brown slacks and cream dress shirt, he still looked like something out of an Abercrombie & Fitch commercial. He had a butt you could bounce quarters off and not even those preppy pants could hide that. She glanced down at his brown loafers and smirked. The man didn't know how to dress for the country. "Depends."

He followed her gaze and frowned. "Depends on what?"

"On how I'm feeling that day. Sometimes it's an on-time day and sometimes it just isn't. You can guess what kind of day today is."

"What were you smiling at?"

"I wasn't smiling, I was smirking."

"Fine. What were you *smirking* about? Is there something wrong with my shoes?"

She cocked her head at him. "Just an odd choice for someone who's going to tromp through thistles and ragweed. I prefer good old-fashioned hiking boots." She lifted her foot and modeled her worn shoe. "But that's just me. City folks tend to do things differently I'm told."

"Oh, I get it. You're playing the wise country local while I'm playing the part of idiot city guy who wouldn't know a poison-oak branch from a manzanita bush."

She arched her brow. "Do you?"

"Of course I do," he retorted, but she caught his eyes darting to the side a bit nervously. "Poison oak has bright green leaves and manzanita has sticky red berries attached."

"Not bad, professor, but what about in the winter? What does poison oak look like then?" He faltered and she grinned, affecting a country-bumpkin stereotype voice. "Well, mister, when it's winter time pois'n oak looks like plain ole sticks, but if'n you touch 'em, you're still gonna be in a world of hurt 'cuz it still has the oils that cause the 'llergic reaction."

"Cute."

"I thought so."

"Thanks for the botany lesson. Can we get to work now?"

"You're the boss." She pulled a rolled-up

chunk of paper from her back pocket and handed it to him. She supposed she could've finessed the presentation, but she liked to keep her work with her at all times and packing around a clipboard wasn't always convenient to the way her mind operated. He unfurled the papers with an air of exasperation and her mouth itched to smile. How anyone could be so uptight was beyond her but it was fun watching him loosen up.

While he studied her plans, her imagination ran a little wild wondering what he'd look like in a pair of faded jeans, no shirt and nicely mussed bed-head. Her toes curled and her fingers tingled in anticipation of an event that she'd never allow to happen. She shook her hands, annoyed at herself and the sensation.

"What's wrong?" he asked.

"Nothing," she said too quickly, shuddering at the idea of sharing that crazy thought. "What do you think of the plans?"

His gaze returned reluctantly to the papers in his hand. "Aside from the proliferation of flowers everywhere, they look suitable for what I'm going for."

"Well, I told you I wasn't going for the desert look. Flowers sell houses, makes them look homey and welcoming."

He made a noncommittal noise but otherwise didn't protest, and after rolling the papers in a column, he tucked them under his arm. "Shall we commence the walk-through?"

"Are you sure? In those shoes?"

"Just lead the way."

"Fine, but if you end up with poison oak in an unmentionable place, don't go blaming me. If I have to drag you out of a patch my rate's going to go up exponentially."

He grimaced. "Duly noted. I'll do my best to stay on my feet."

"Good."

BEN FELL IN STEP with Nora. Irritation at her attitude fueled his stride until he happened to catch the view of her backside. Plump and pert and clad lovingly in khaki cargo pants, it was all he could do not to stare. He stumbled on a rock partially hidden by over-grown weeds and she slowed.

"You okay?"

"Fine," he answered, his cheeks flaring. "I'm right behind you. Where are we going by the way?"

She high stepped the tall grass as she talked, the movement of her legs sending his imagination into overdrive. His frustration returned, only this time it was directed at himself. Her voice jerked him to attention.

"I'm not sure if you saw it in my plans, but I'd like to define the trail that leads down to the creek. Right now it's just a deer path, but I think it would add to the ambience if there was a lighted stairway. People love to know they have their own little spot on the creek. Of course, since the river feeds this part of the creek, the water runs all year, which is another draw."

"Good to know." He glanced down at his slacks. They were covered in an assortment of sticky weeds. The pungent odor from the crushed foliage was oddly enjoyable, though he wasn't sure his slacks would ever recover. "This hill is pretty steep. You sure that's a good idea?"

She spared him an indulgent look. "Of course I do."

The sight of the lazily winding creek glistening below brought up treasured memories, ones he kept under lock and key because they weren't tainted by his parents. His time with Nora seemed unreal, as if he'd dreamed it in an attempt to escape the sound of his mother crying and his father beating her down with his words as much as his hands. It was part of the reason Ben hadn't said anything to Nora, but keeping the secret weighed on him in a way he hadn't anticipated. It needed to be out in the open so they could move on. Sounded simple enough, but the only problem was that he hadn't a clue how to tell her. The purest opportunity passed him by days ago. Deciding to try a casual approach, he gestured to the creek. "You ever go down there anymore?"

In hindsight, he realized casual hadn't been the right choice. Though if he really gave it some thought, sinking to his knees in apology probably wouldn't have worked either.

She sucked in a sharp breath and swore softly as a storm built behind her eyes.

"Hold on…" He started in alarm at how quickly her temper kindled. "Let's not make a mountain out of a molehill."

"You haven't seen the half of it," she said, her eyes flashing. "You pretended that you didn't remember me but I knew it!" She swore again and bracketed her hips with her hands, drawing his gaze to her nicely spanned waist until he realized he was enjoying the view a little too much. "Why? Why would you do that? Do you have any idea how long I've been stressed out over this stupid thing? My God, I can't believe I let myself get sucked into your little game."

"I wasn't playing a game," he tried assuring her. Apologize. It was the right thing to do, his mind instructed, but his mouth didn't obey. "I just didn't feel it was relevant to the job."

She sputtered. "Not relevant? Perhaps not, but it would've been decent of you to admit that you remembered me instead of acting like you'd never laid eyes on me before. That was mean, if you ask me."

"Well I didn't ask you, and judging by your reaction it's a damn good thing I didn't. I don't have time for drama, Ms. Simmons. I hired you because you're the best in the area. I was impressed with your portfolio and despite your oddities, I'm amenable to continuing this relationship if you'll agree to stop with the histrionics."

"Spare me your benevolence. You can take your double-sided compliments and shove them, Benjamin Scott Hollister III." He startled at her use of his full name but she continued, snatching the plans from his hands and shoving them into her back pocket again. "Your opinion of my work means nothing to me. I agreed to take the job because I thought highly of your grandparents, but not even my regard for B.J. and Corrinda can change the fact that you're a jerk. Find yourself someone else to fix the yard. I quit."

Caught off guard at her unexpected announcement, he realized things had gone too far. His brain screamed for damage control and he caught her arm before she managed to stomp away. "Where are you going? We need to talk this out," he said, striving for calm.

She yanked her arm, but he held it firm. "Let go."

"Not until you agree to talk rationally about this."

"I said let go!"

She gave a savage jerk of her arm, ripping it out of his grasp, the violence of the movement sending him off balance and teetering dangerously on the rocky terrain.

"Nora!" he managed to gasp, and she turned just in time to watch in wide-eyed surprise as he went tumbling down the steep embankment. He tried to protect his body, but his side connected with a half-buried rock and a damp crack sent stars bursting behind his eyes.

SECONDS MAY HAVE PASSED before Nora sprang into horrified action, but it felt as if time had slowed to a crawl as she watched Ben's body tumble and flop down the embankment, gathering momentum as he headed toward the creek that was swollen with the winter-snow runoff until he finally stopped a hairbreadth away from smacking his head on a slab of granite.

"Oh God, Ben," she breathed, scrambling down the hillside to reach him, her heart thudding painfully as she cursed her temper and her mouth. "Please don't be dead. *Please* don't be dead!"

Her stomach pitched dangerously at the sight of Ben's cuts and contusions. Blood seeped from a deep gash in his forehead. She fought the dizziness that never failed to come whenever she was faced with the sight of blood and closed her eyes to clear her vision. Now was not the time to faint. The wave passed and she opened her eyes, moving closer to Ben in search of some kind of sign that she hadn't just killed him with her temper.

She dropped to her knees and gently pressed her fingers to his wrist. A steady heartbeat thumped softly and she exhaled in relief. He wasn't dead, but judging by his obvious injuries, when he woke up he might want to be.

Ben groaned and she winced at the pain couched inside the sound.

"Don't move," she whispered, pulling her cell phone from her back pocket to dial 911. He groaned again and she slipped her hand into his and gave it a gentle squeeze to let him know he wasn't alone while she waited impatiently for the operator. His eyes remained shut but the moaning stopped. An operator came on the line and Nora wasted little time in telling the man what had happened.

"We're down at the creek below the Hollister house. Hurry, he's hurt pretty bad. I think he may have broken something." *Or everything*, she thought worriedly, wincing at the mess Ben had become during his trip down the hill. His previously beautiful shirt was ripped and torn, the fine fabric completely trashed, and he was missing one shoe. "Please hurry."

"They're on their way," the dispatcher assured her as the line clicked off.

Nora bit her lip, never before faced with a situation like this. "Stupid shoes. Who wears loafers in the mountains?" she grumbled, but fear overrode her pique. Why did she jerk her arm like that? She'd known they were too close to the edge but her temper got the best of her. No, a voice reprimanded sternly, not temper—mostly pride. She'd been humiliated by his omission.

Ben's eyes fluttered open, pain darkening the soft green until he squeezed them shut again. "Damn," he muttered from between clenched teeth. "Nora?"

"I'm here. Try not to move around. An ambulance is coming," she said, her guilt tripling when he grunted against the pain, his chest moving in short, stilted motions. "You lost your shoe somewhere," she said, searching for something to say. "I'll buy you a new one."

"Screw the shoe," he said. "Where's that ambulance?"

"Be patient, they're on their way. We're not in the city, so it's not like they're just around the corner. Besides, if you hadn't been so damn pushy this wouldn't have happened. For future reference, I don't like to be—" The sound of the ambulance cut her off, which was probably a good thing because her nerves had taken hold of her mouth. Paramedics appeared at the top of the small ridge and hollered down to them.

"Who's the victim?" a tall, curvy woman questioned in a clear voice. Nora gestured to Ben and the woman disappeared only to reappear with reinforcements in the way of firefighters carrying an orange stretcher.

The woman called out. "Do you need help, too?"

"No, *I* wore appropriate shoes for the day," she answered, but the woman only stared. Nora waved her away. "I'll sit with him until the firefighters get down here."

"Fine."

Moments later, two firefighters were roped and anchored to the top while they were lowered to Ben and Nora's position. Nora scooted carefully out of the way and, while they loaded him onto the stretcher, she made the climb back up, huffing a little with the exertion by the time she got to the top.

The firefighters pulled Ben over the edge of the ridge and the paramedics took over. The woman who'd first called out to them wasn't anyone Nora knew, but she seemed to know her job.

"At least one broken rib, possibly bruised lung and a fractured ankle." She turned to Nora. "What happened?"

"He fell."

The woman made a sound of annoyance. "I gathered that. How did he fall?"

The woman was just doing her job, but explaining what happened only served to make Nora feel worse. She glared. "The usual way. He went ass over teakettle until he stopped at the edge of that big rock. What difference does it make to his treatment how he fell exactly?"

A sheriff cruiser appeared on the scene and the woman smiled thinly. "It makes a big difference to them. I'd say it's the difference between attempted murder and an accident."

Nora gaped. Who would think that she'd try to purposefully hurt someone like that? It wasn't as if she had a history of pushing people down mountains. Mike Curtis, an older deputy who'd gone to school with her dad, approached them.

"What happened here?" he asked, taking a moment to spit a stream of chewing-tobacco juice on the dusty ground. "Heard on the radio someone took a spill."

"Mike," Nora said, glad someone was here who'd show this newcomer how things were done in Emmett's Mill. "Thank God you're here. My friend Ben fell and this woman is acting like I pushed him or something."

"Now, Dana, that's no way to make friends," he admonished, and the woman snorted and climbed into the back of the ambulance just before it took off, siren blaring. He chuckled. "She's a live one. Gotta love her, though. How you doing, Little Gerry?"

Nora gave him a stony look for calling her the nickname he'd picked for her years ago because, according to him, she was just like her father, Gerald. In other words, stubborn, obstinate and ornery on the best of days. "I was fine until Ben decided to go off-roading with his face. Who is that woman anyway?"

"Dana Collins. New to the area. Just got hired on a few weeks ago. She has a relative here or something housed over at Laurel Manor Senior Center. I only know about her because I heard Samuel Halvorsen had dated her for a spell."

Nora forgot all about Ben and stared at Mike. "What? No. Sammy would've told me. We're pretty close. He's never not shared who he's seeing."

"Be that as it may, I have it on pretty good authority that Sammy and Dana were sweet on each other…at least for a while. Don't know what happened, but I suspect the same thing that always happens with that boy." He shook his head as he walked away. "He's in love with the *idea* of being in love."

She wanted to defend her best friend but there was some truth to Mike's statement. Sammy loved the hunt, not the prize. But the bigger question was, why hadn't he told her about this Dana woman? As Nora headed for her truck to go to the hospital, she answered her own question—Sammy must've been trying to tell her the other night, but she'd been too wrapped up in her own troubles to pay attention. What had he said? She jumped into the truck and started the engine. She sat up straighter. He'd said something about wanting more out of a relationship. Oh, Sammy, she wanted to moan, peeling out of the driveway. You really know how to pick 'em.

# CHAPTER SIX

NORA WALKED INTO the emergency room of the small hospital and went straight to the only closed curtain. She could hear her family physician, his voice low and gravelly and oddly soothing, and knew he was talking about Ben to the nurse.

She pushed aside the curtain and slipped inside, ignoring Dr. Hessle's expression as the nurse left them alone. "Did you have something to do with this, young lady?" he asked gravely.

Nora avoided his stare and squirmed a little. Doc Hessle had had an ability to see into her conscience that he'd honed over the many years filled with cuts, broken bones and contusions. They weren't always her own injuries, but she was most certainly involved in some way or another.

"Who wears loafers in the mountains?" she retorted, and a subtle smile crept onto his aged face, and she knew no matter what she said, he wouldn't hold it against her. Nora was Doc Hessle's favorite patient. Nora's mom, Missy, used to joke that he liked Nora the best because she helped pay for his second home with all her hospital visits. "Is he going to be okay?" she asked in all seriousness.

"Eventually," he replied with a nod. "Pretty banged up. You didn't push him down that hill, did you?"

Nora gasped. "Doc! You know me better than that. You must've been talking to that new paramedic, Dana something or another. She and I are going to have words real soon, I promise you that."

"Leave her alone, she's our best paramedic. I don't want you scaring her off. Besides, I know you better than most and I know you've got a wicked temper." He grinned. "It's the best part of your personality. But this boy is hurt bad. It's just as Dana said—broken rib, bruised lung and a fractured ankle. Who is he?"

"Ben Hollister," Nora answered, her gaze skittering away from the puffy gash on his head. "Remember B.J. and Corrinda? He's their grandson. He inherited the house."

Doc Hessle nodded. "That explains him, what about you?"

Nora groaned. "Doc, let's just say I'm not

completely innocent and I feel really bad about it, so please drop it."

He chuckled and Ben stirred, his eyes opening slowly. "How you feeling, son? Those pain meds kick in yet?"

Ben paused as if checking for any aches and nodded carefully. "No pain, just tired," he said, his voice husky and very sexy, which she realized was incredibly inappropriate given the situation, but since it was in the privacy of her own mind, she simply enjoyed the guilty pleasure. "What's the prognosis?" he asked, his perfectly set hair askew.

"Your rib and lung will heal on their own in a few weeks, provided you don't do anything strenuous. The ankle is another matter. It's a rather bad break. I'm going to have to recommend that you stay off it for at least six weeks."

The medicine-induced haze cleared from his eyes as he shook his head. "That's going to be hard to do, Doctor. I don't live in Emmett's Mill and the only person I know here is Nora." He met Nora's gaze briefly before going back to the doctor. "I'm an attorney in the Bay Area and I have a job to return to."

"Fine by me, but do you have someone who can drive you, help around the house and ensure that you don't put pressure on that foot?"

"Is that really necessary?"

"Do you want to walk again?"

He blanched. "Of course I do."

"Then you'll find a way to stay off that foot." Doc Hessle gathered his clipboard in front of his stomach and gestured toward Nora. "I heard you inherited your grandparents' house, so you have a place you could hole up in while you recuperate. Nora here could help out I'm sure."

Nora caught Doc Hessle's last statement and nearly swallowed her tongue as she protested his suggestion. "I have clients...lots of them Doc. I can't take time off to play nursemaid. Sorry. Not really my forte."

Doc Hessle raised an assessing eyebrow at them both and then turned to Nora. "This boy needs help and you're the only person he knows. Don't make your mama turn over in her grave, young lady. Where's your manners?"

"He's not a boy," Nora muttered, shooting Ben a mutinous look. "And he has a life to get back to." Chagrined by Doc Hessle's disappointed expression, she looked to Ben for backup. Surely he didn't want her for a nursemaid, either. As she'd already proven, she wasn't the caregiving type—that was

Natalie's area of expertise. Nora was more of the get-mad-push-a-guy-off-a-cliff type.

Ben drew a deep breath and thanked the doctor for patching him up but Nora read more than irritation in his eyes. She caught a moment of bleakness that immediately poked at the soft spot in her heart, which she did her damnedest to cover most of the time, and she realized how alone he felt. If the situation were reversed, Nora couldn't imagine being without her family in a town full of strangers. "Maybe you should call your parents," she said, fishing for information as much as making a helpful suggestion.

"I'm a little old to be running home to Mommy, don't you think?" he said.

"No one's too old for the love and care of their parents—especially from their mommy, as you put it. I'd give anything to have my mom here with me again, but I don't have that option. She died last year." Ben's expression faltered and he mumbled an apology, which she waved away. "You didn't kill her, cancer did. But what I'm getting from your comment is that your parents aren't exactly the kind you can turn to. Am I right?"

He gave a grudging jerk of his head, then shifted uncomfortably in the small hospital bed to say a bit snappishly, "Not everyone has the Walton house to grow up in."

"More's the pity," Doc Hessle interjected with a sad sigh, eyeing Ben speculatively before looking at Nora with expectation. "Well? What's it going to be, young lady?"

Nora ignored the doc and turned to Ben in earnest. "So, who can you get to care for you in the Bay Area? A friend, perhaps. Maybe a girlfriend?"

His eyes shut. "No girlfriend and no one I'd consider calling in this particular instance." He opened his eyes again but chose to stare past Nora. The disconcerting way he refused to meet her gaze made her wonder what kind of sterile life he was living. "I have a maid but she doesn't speak English," he said. "The firm pays for her services."

"You don't have any friends?" Nora asked curiously. "No one? Who do you hang out with when you're not working? What about weekends? Holidays?"

He glared as if angry at her for pointing out how sad that sounded and then looked at Doc Hessle who'd been watching the exchange with an expression of mild amusement. For the life of her, Nora couldn't see anything remotely amusing about the situation, and asked, "When can Ben get out of here?"

"His discharge paperwork will be ready in a few minutes I suspect," he answered, handing Ben a prescription for more pain meds.

Ben nodded in grim satisfaction and closed his eyes again, giving Nora the distinct impression he'd just dismissed both her and Doc Hessle. A frown replaced the doc's amusement and he narrowed his bushy-browed gaze at Ben much as he would at a surly teen. Nora had been on the receiving end of that look more times than she wanted to count and didn't envy Ben.

"Being as I knew your grandparents to be fine folk, I'll only say this one thing and then get out of your hair," Doc Hessle began, the authority in his tone jerking Ben to attention. "You're seriously injured and you need someone to help you out. I suggest you look at the blessings, odd as they may seem, that are right in front of your damn nose." Ben opened his mouth to offer a rebuttal no doubt, but Doc Hessle didn't give him the chance. This time it was Ben who was dismissed as Doc Hessle walked away grousing under his breath.

"Way to go." Nora smirked. "Now I know why you don't have any friends."

"I said I don't have friends in the Bay Area," he snapped.

"Fine, then you'd better get on the horn and call up those long-distance friends of yours so they can care for your sorry ass, or else you're going to have to learn a second language so that you can communicate your needs to your maid."

Ben looked ready to throw out another scathing remark, but apparently thought better of it, closing his mouth and shaking his head. "This is great timing," he muttered. "Ah, hell."

Guilt crept up and tapped her on the shoulder, and despite her efforts to shrug it off, she was reminded of the part she'd played in Ben's injuries. He couldn't—or wouldn't—call his parents. No friends. A foreign maid who didn't speak a lick of English. And he was basically crippled for the next six weeks.

He could afford to hire someone, the rational side of her brain reminded her, but it didn't matter, the crazy side had already won control and her mouth was moving before she realized what she was saying.

"Alright, here's the deal. You hired me to do the landscaping, I suppose since I'll already be there, I can help out a bit if you decide to stay for a while."

Ben stared at her, not quite sure he heard correctly.

"Well, don't look at me like I lost my mind or something," she grumbled, "because it already feels like I did and I don't need you to rub it in."

It must be the pain meds. They were messing with his brain. Surely Nora hadn't just suggested he stay here while she cared for him. A ripple passed through his numbed body and he jerked against the implications. "No," he stated flatly. "I can't let you do that."

"Why not?"

Because of all the dumb things he could possibly do, letting a woman he was clearly attracted to—in the most baffling way possible—care for him begged for trouble he didn't want to invite into his life. "Because it's ridiculous for one, and two, it would be unprofessional."

After a moment of consideration, she countered, "Not if you paid me."

"Paid you?"

"Yeah, paid me. You're going to end up paying someone to care for you anyway, why not me? That should take care of any weird interpersonal issues. Besides, I'll be working on the house and coming in and out, so I can easily pop in wherever you're sitting and check on you. As much as I was against it in the beginning, now I see the sense in it."

*At least one of us can,* he wanted to grouse. Her suggestion made sense on paper but when put into practice fell apart because certain emotions, in this case, inappropriate curiosity, mucked things up. But she did make a valuable point. He was still muddling through the logistics of such an arrangement when Dr. Hessle returned and gave the two of them an assessing look that Nora capitalized on.

"I've agreed to look after Ben while he's recuperating," she told him, although Ben hadn't actually accepted her offer.

"Good. Glad you came to your senses," the doctor said, though Ben wasn't sure whom he was addressing. "A nurse will come in a few moments to put a cast on that ankle, and once it's set Nora can take you home but I would like you to come back in about two weeks so I can check that rib. Remember, off your feet."

The doctor left the curtained area and Ben was left with Nora. "You don't have to drive me," he started, feeling more awkward than he'd ever felt in his life. "I can get a taxi or something."

"Sure, and while you're at it, why don't you order up some Thai food to go." His blank stare prompted her to explain in annoyance, "We don't have a taxi service or a Thai-food restaurant. You can't walk to your grandparents' house, so I'll take you."

"I don't want you to go out of your way," he said glumly. "I'll figure something out."

"Don't be stupid. I'll drive you."

A smiling nurse entered, pushing a cart filled with casting materials and Ben swallowed the retort on his tongue. It was probably better he hadn't let his mouth take over at this point. While he wasn't keen on climbing into a car with the same woman who'd nearly killed him even if it was by accident, she made a good point. Without any transportation and an inability to drive, he was stuck.

The nurse gestured to the material with an apologetic expression. "Pink or blue? We seem to be out of the plain white we usually use for adults," she said, and out of the corner of his eye, Ben caught Nora grinning.

"Blue," he sighed.

"Oh, I don't know, they say real men wear pink," Nora joked.

Ben cut Nora a short look. "This man doesn't."

She shrugged, but she was practically vibrating from the laughter she was holding back. "Suit yourself," she said.

"Blue it is, then," the nurse said, settling beside Ben to start the process.

Fifteen minutes later, Ben's ankle was cast in blue plaster gauze, and another ten minutes later, it was hard as a rock. He could already feel an itch in a place he wouldn't be able to reach for the next six weeks and he wanted to curse the situation up one side and down the other, but he settled for getting the hell out of there. The nurse left and Ben swung his leg over the side of the bed.

"Let me at least give you some gas money," he offered gruffly, hating how helpless he felt.

"Fine. I'll go get someone so we can wheel you out of here. I'm starving."

Moments later Nora returned with a surly-looking male nurse who looked ready to stuff him in the wheelchair he was pushing just for the sake of doing it. Nora must've pulled him away from a break.

"Paul is going to wheel you out front, and I'll meet you there with my truck." Nora didn't wait for him to agree or disagree and was gone in a blink.

Ben eyed Paul. "Did she interrupt something?"

"My dinner."

He grimaced. "Not my idea. Try not to take it out on me."

Paul's expression didn't change and Ben was thankful he was still doped up on pain meds. Instinct told him Paul wasn't in the mood to be gentle.

THE AWKWARD SILENCE was nearly unbearable, but Nora suffered through it, telling herself penance was never a picnic. Several times the nippy draft coming from the outside caused Ben to shiver, reminding her that he was made from different stock and accustomed to different things—such as vehicles that didn't require a wrench to roll up the passenger-side window—and wondered if her sanity was on permanent hiatus, or if it was bound to return before she did something really stupid.

She slid a surreptitious glance his way, taking in the strong angles of his silhouette in the darkened cab, and realized a part of her—that ridiculously breathy and girlie part—was curious to see what kind of mischief they could make together.

*Keep it together, Simmons*. She'd caused enough damage for one day.

She pulled into Ben's driveway and

hopped from her side to help him out. His clenched jaw could've been from the pain meds wearing off or that she was snugged up to him as she helped him from the truck so they could manage an odd hop and lean to the front door.

"This is ridiculous," he grunted, breathing hard against the exertion. "We should've waited until I could've found some crutches."

"I already told you, I asked around when I went to get the truck. The medical-supply closet at the hospital was locked and the guy with the key had already gone home. So suck it up and get to hopping—you're killing my shoulder!"

Nora focused on getting him up the short steps to the front door and not on the mix of scents assaulting her nostrils, scents that if pressed, she'd have to admit were annoyingly arousing. Fresh dirt, the faint cling of crushed grass and the tease of some expensive cologne played with her senses, and she gritted her teeth against the desire to bury her nose in the crook of his neck...or somewhere else on his hard body. If all lawyers were built like Ben, she might've adjusted her opinion about them a long time ago.

"Can you hop any faster?" she grunted, irritation with herself making her surly.

"Sorry my hopping skills aren't up to your standards," he retorted as they both wobbled on the last step. "Can you hold steady before you break my other ankle?"

Nora stiffened, tempted to drop him for that comment, but swallowed her impulse. She was trying to do a good thing and she wasn't going to let his attitude derail her. Ben pulled away and struggled to hop on his own to the front door. She watched in sardonic amusement as he tried to keep his balance without her. Nora's mom used to say you couldn't help someone who didn't want your help, but she didn't say anything about not being able to laugh at their dumb ass when they fell on it.

Ben stopped and steadied himself with his right arm against the doorjamb and fished in his pocket for the key, but Nora saw that the strength in the leg holding up his ankle was flagging. Stupid pride, she thought with exasperation, knowing he was seconds away from losing that battle. But pride was something she understood and even as she was tempted just to take the key and open the door to save him from himself, she waited.

Nora recognized Ben's need to be self-sufficient despite his obvious need for help. She'd fought that battle her entire childhood.

Carving an identity for herself against two older sisters and an overbearing father had left its share of battle wounds. Seeing something similar in Ben made her appreciate there was more to the man than what she'd been ready to believe.

He finally managed to get the key in the lock and once the door was open, she slipped under his arm and he let her help him inside.

## CHAPTER SEVEN

THE NEXT MORNING Ben lay in the double bed where he'd spent a restless night, and despite the sunlight streaming through the window of the master suite, he felt panic at his predicament.

Nora had been right—he had no one to call upon for help. He was alone in this world, surrounded by people who'd love to watch him fall, simply for the entertainment value of seeing him break into a million pieces.

Ben hadn't made friends at the firm purposefully. He didn't want to give anyone the power to stab him in the back later. He kept to himself and made work his life. Crossing his forearms across his eyes, he blocked out the sunlight and the fear that smothered his confidence and reminded him that, in hindsight, his choices were to blame for his loneliness.

No, Nora was to blame for this. The insidious voice whispered in his head, and while it was easier to accept that counsel, he knew it wasn't entirely true. He shouldn't have grabbed her. He'd acted like a self-righteous prig with a woman who had a flash-burn temper, and now he was paying her to help him out. The irony was disturbing.

He winced as his side pulled, but when he tried to suck a deep breath against the burn, his bruised lung protested and he rolled onto his undamaged side and concentrated on taking slow, shallow breaths until the stars spinning around his head faded and disappeared. What was he going to tell the firm? What about the Wallace case? He needed the case files, needed to make contact with Ed and let him know of the situation, not that the bastard would give a damn. From what Ben had seen, Ed Wallace had turned in his heart in exchange for lots of money. Ben bounced his head against the flat pillow in frustration and growled. He had to find a way to fix this before he ended up without a job and nowhere to go.

NORA ARRIVED at Ben's place around 9:00 a.m. with a brown bag filled with groceries, well, edible foodstuff like packaged doughnuts and coffee packets just in case Ben was the type who needed a pick-me-up in the morning, and bounded the stairs to the front door.

She was in good spirits despite getting up earlier than she preferred and detoured to the kitchen before heading into the bedroom, where she knocked twice and entered without thinking.

Boy, there was a reason her mom always said to wait for permission before opening a closed door. Ben stood haphazardly clutching a towel much too small for his wide frame across his lean hips, his hair wet and dripping. She gaped at the six-pack of muscle cording his stomach and daring her to follow the happy trail of dark hair that disappeared behind the towel and teased her with the promise of what lay beneath. Not even the motley bruising around his injured rib did much to ruin the view and she was mortified to note if she stared any harder, her pointed gaze might pierce his skin and pop out the other side.

"Oh!" She spun around, her cheeks hot enough to catch the drapes on fire, and mentally counted to ten to give her heart a chance to begin beating again. "I...I...didn't think...well, of course, I should've waited... oh, God!"

Nora heard his labored breathing and the springs on the bed creak as it absorbed Ben's weight. Showering must've been terribly difficult, she realized. A shadow of concern managed to override her embarrassment long enough for her to ask tentatively, "Hey, are you okay?"

There was a long pause and then, "Yeah, uh, I'm fine, just a little winded. And exposed," he added unnecessarily. She bit her lip and cursed silently for not thinking before she opened that door. But, oh goodness, the man was hot. Thanks to that tantalizing snapshot her dreams were bound to be bothersome.

He exhaled softly then ground out, "I think I need your help."

"What kind of help?" she asked warily, not sure she trusted herself not to pet him like an exotic animal if she got too close.

"I can't get my pants on," he admitted, and by his tone she could almost see his own cheeks reddening. "I guess I didn't think this through, but I had dirt in my hair and grass stains on my palms and had to wash up."

"How'd you manage to shower with your cast?" she asked, careful to keep her eyes focused straight ahead and nowhere near where she might catch another glimpse of his naked skin.

"I wrapped it in a plastic bag and taped it off. It's not perfect, but I couldn't stand going to bed another night covered in dirt and sweat."

She nodded. That made sense, even if it wasn't the smartest thing to do. He could've fallen in the shower or something. She looked around as she asked, "What happened to the loose hospital trousers you were wearing last night?"

"Uh, they ripped when I was trying to get them off." He added defensively, "They were made of very thin cotton."

Nora drew a deep breath and slowly turned, hoping he was covered with a blanket so she didn't humiliate herself further by drooling. A mixture of relief and chagrin washed over her when she saw the lower half of his body was hidden from view by the faded quilt on the bed.

"Is that it?" As if that wasn't enough, she wanted to snap. "Help you get dressed?"

"No, I have one more thing to ask," he admitted.

"Which is?"

He adjusted his body with slow, deliberate movements and she caught his wince but didn't comment. She didn't think he would appreciate coddling, which was fine by

Nora—coddling didn't come naturally to her anyway. Ben settled into his new position carefully then met her wary gaze.

"I need you to drive me to my place in San Francisco so I can make arrangements, get clothes and forward my mail for the next six weeks."

HE KNEW HIS REQUEST wouldn't go over well, but honestly, how was he supposed to hole up in Emmett's Mill without provisions? At least he had to pick up his work files and some clothes.

Her face screwed into an annoyed frown but she didn't protest. "I suppose that's reasonable," she said. "But I'm not sure if my truck is up to driving to the city. Usually when I have trips farther than Coldwater or Sonora, I borrow a friend's truck. It's newer and doesn't threaten to die after a few miles. I guess I can ask to borrow it for this trip."

"You can drive my car," he said.

"Your car?" she repeated, her expression pensive. "You'd trust me to drive that fancy sports car?"

"Is there some reason why I shouldn't? Can you drive stick?"

"Of course."

"All right then. I don't see a problem."

Nora worried her bottom lip, taking a long moment to mull over his offer and then reluctantly agreed.

Her hesitation surprised him. So Nora Simmons *wasn't* fearless. He understood her apprehension. There was something heady about slipping behind the wheel of a seventy-five-thousand-dollar vehicle. He didn't have long to savor the moment, though, as her demeanor changed as she gestured toward him.

"Okay, so that's settled, but what are we going to do about your pants? Your old ones are ripped and ruined, and as far as I know you don't have a spare pair in the closet. I'm sure as hell not driving you into the city wearing just your underwear."

"I have a pair of sweats in the trunk of the car." He picked up the keys from the nightstand and tossed them to her. She caught them neatly and he further instructed, "Just bring the entire gym bag. I keep spare toiletries in there, as well."

"Of course you do," she muttered. "Late-night gym visits? Or rather early-morning emergency supplies for that *all-nighter?*"

"A little of both," he admitted with a discomfited chuckle before she spun on her heel and left him. The odd spurt of jealousy flashing in her gray eyes made his groin tighten. There wasn't a word in the English dictionary to describe that woman, but his body didn't care. Those were matters of the brain; his body reacted to something else entirely.

The next six weeks could be hell—or one wild ride.

# CHAPTER EIGHT

SAMMY POUNDED BACK another beer, trying to tune out the sound of Dana's laughter. She was having a good time with her ambulance buddies in the corner of the bar, and he'd been miserable since she left him.

What was wrong with him? He'd only known her a handful of months since she'd come to town but she was unlike any woman with whom he'd ever shared a bed. Just thinking about those golden moments made his guts twist and roll at the knowledge he'd screwed it all up with one idiotic move.

What was so special about her? he thought bitterly, hating this new development in his brain, wishing and waiting for the familiar feeling of ambivalence to return when a relationship came to an end. He was Sammy Halvorsen, an infamous player in the love game. His dad used to joke Sammy could charm the good sense out of any woman faster than a few cocktails. The ladies didn't seem to mind. He was upfront and honest with them and everyone had a good time.

Until now.

He stole a glance her way, his heart aching for what he couldn't have. She wasn't what usually turned his head. Too tall, too skinny and brunette. Did he mention smart? Yeah, she was that, too. Too smart to put up with his crap, apparently.

The bar was loud, but he could still pick out the sound of her voice from the crowded table. Her laugh was full of the confidence she exuded from every pore, and while at first glance she wasn't the kind of girl who turned heads, one look from her sultry brown eyes and Sammy's head had nearly swiveled off his shoulders.

He tipped his beer in a sullen motion, finishing it in one loud swallow, and decided he didn't want to listen anymore, didn't want to drink himself into a stupor to numb the pain, and damn well didn't want to pretend he was the same as he ever was.

Slanting a look her way, willing her to see him yet trying to be invisible, his blood heated when he saw one of the guys at her table sling an arm casually around the back of her chair. Sammy swallowed a snarl and forced himself to look away.

As much as he wanted to act the same as always, he'd changed and he blamed her. He hated the foreign feelings crowding his thoughts and making him surly and hard to be around. Even his older brother, Dean, a man not known for his verbosity had a few choice words for him the other day when Sammy had snapped at another worker on the job site. All he could think of was her and how cold his bed seemed without her—and by the looks of it, she could really care less.

*Screw this.*

He rose from the stool on stiff legs and headed for the door.

NORA HELD OPEN the apartment door for Ben so that he could maneuver his crutches through, and then followed him inside the tidy residence.

"Make yourself comfortable," he said, moving slowly into what she assumed was his bedroom. "I'll just be a minute."

"Make it a Manhattan minute," she grumbled, not quite sure why she'd agreed to this little excursion. It was bad enough she was his makeshift nurse, now she was his chauffeur? Nora harrumphed, and let her gaze wander the living room, taking immediate note of how bare and spartan the place looked. Every countertop shone as if it'd been buffed and waxed and the brushed stainless-steel refrigerator matched the fixtures. Perfectly contrasting throw pillows in no-nonsense materials sat at attention on the luxurious soft black microfiber sofa as if they were glued to the surface, and the floor was immaculate. Not a speck of dust, an errant lint ball, not even a dead plant leaf anywhere in sight.

"Your maid may not speak English, but she keeps your house like a mortuary," she observed out loud, then clarified silently that it was more like a museum. A museum dedicated to the barren corporate existence of a man who never actually lived.

She glanced at the smooth, clutter-free surfaces in the living room and frowned. Not a single photo to liven up the place.

"Are you sure you live here?" she asked.

"What?" he hollered from the back.

"Nothing. What are you doing back there?"

"Packing a few essentials. Take a load off. Have a seat."

Where? Nothing looked as if it was made for sitting. The place looked more like a designer showroom than an area where you could pop a squat and relax. Just being there made her shoulders tense. For a moment she tried hard to imagine Ben kicking back on a Sunday morning, newspaper in hand, hair all rumpled, in anything less somber than a three-piece suit, but her imagination went a little overboard and stripped him down to boxers, a silk robe and a wicked, sexy-as-hell, come-hither grin before she put an immediate stop to her mental wandering with an annoyed growl. Who she was growling at—her or him—she couldn't be sure. All she knew was that seeing him trying to shield himself from her view with a worn piece of fabric that looked more like a hand towel had whipped her brain into a frenzy of inappropriate and irritating mental imagery. Spending an entire car ride in such proximity had only made things worse.

Thirsty, Nora stalked to the fridge and peered inside, shocked to see it full of food. She half expected it to be devoid of anything more substantial than a box of baking soda, much like the apartment itself. An image of Ben in the kitchen, cooking gourmet meals—judging by the ingredients stocked—popped into her head and she batted her hand as if that alone could dislodge the direction of her thoughts. Things had been a lot less complicated a week ago. Hell, one morning ago, she amended before eyeing a Corona and grabbing it.

She opened it and looked for a trash can but couldn't find one. Ben hobbled into the room and found her searching. He pointed to a small machine built into the counter. Ah, of course—trash compactor. She pulled out the tray and dropped the top inside.

"Got some fancy stuff here," she commented as he moved past her into the living room to sit down. "Did you buy out the IKEA catalog when you furnished your apartment?"

"I like clean lines and uncluttered space," he said by way of explanation. "I find it hard to concentrate when things are a mess."

He'd probably lose his mind at her place. Not that she'd ever invite him. "Do you consider pictures clutter?" she asked.

"No, I just never got around to hanging some. Unlike you, I'm an only child. A bunch of pictures of me on the walls seemed a little odd."

The barest hint of a smile edged his mouth and she reacted with one of her own. "So you do have a sense of humor buried under that three-piece-suit demeanor of yours. I was beginning to worry."

"You? Worry about me? I wouldn't hear of it."

"Have you always been such a smart-ass or is this something you save just for me?"

His grin widened into something bordering on playful and Nora was struck by how it changed his face from aloof to warm and engaging. He should do that more often. *No, he shouldn't,* a part of her snapped. More smiles like that could land her in a bad position—like horizontal. "What about your parents?" she blurted, panicked by the feelings erupting in her body and the possibilities that abounded in her unbridled imagination.

All signs of jocularity left his expression. "They're divorced. I rarely see either. We have our own lives and we don't cross the same paths."

*Ouch.* There was a sore spot. "Why?" she asked, deciding to poke at it a bit to see what oozed out. "What's up with your parents?"

"Nothing."

"Don't want to talk about it, huh?"

"How very astute of you," he said dryly. "And here I thought country folk tended to be a little slow."

"Watch it, city boy, or you'll be hobbling back to Emmett's Mill," she warned, but there was no rancor in it. She was enjoying herself. "Seriously, what happened in your family that was so bad that you don't like to talk about it?"

"You don't give up, do you?" He arched one dark slash of brow at her in a weary fashion.

Nora smiled. "You don't know the half of it. Please continue. I'm all ears." She settled into the uncomfortable sofa as best she could and tipped her beer, waiting to see if he'd budge. She didn't really expect him to, but he couldn't fault a girl for trying.

"Nothing out of the ordinary, Nora," he answered, surprising her. "We don't have holiday dinners and get-togethers unless we can't avoid it and when we can't, there's copious amounts of single-malt scotch to get us through the rough patches." He quirked a wry but entirely sad grin at her. "Does that sound like something you'd want to commemorate with pictures and video? Well, I for one, didn't think so. I learned at a very young age that the only person you can depend upon is yourself. And thus far, the principle has served me well."

Nora lost the grip on her cavalier attitude. She knew at times she took her family for granted, which was something she realized when her mother died. But even at her

worst—and she could claim some doozies—
Nora had always known her family would be
there for her. Learning that Ben didn't have
that same assurance made something in her
chest ache. She rubbed absently at her chest
as if she could reach the undefined pain
under her skin and massage it out, but it
remained. "Where's that leave you now
when you need to depend upon a virtual
stranger?"

Ben answered honestly. "Uncomfortable."

"I'll bet," she said softly and swigged her
beer, her thoughts in a jumbled mess. She
wanted to press, to delve deeper into the
private cave of his life, but something held
her back. Maybe it was the silence that hung
between them, filled with questions he didn't
want to answer and she was dying to know;
maybe it was the latent sense that if he didn't
want to share, she shouldn't push. Nora
couldn't say. All she knew was that she
understood his feelings and felt bad that
she'd put him in this situation.

*Not just me! His shoes—*

She closed her eyes against the sound of
her own defensive voice and effectively
silenced it. Her mom used to say Nora was
the worst for taking responsibility for her
actions. Well, Nora decided, not today.

"You got what you need?" she asked, rising to throw away the bottle. As she entered the kitchen, an idea came to her. "You have a paper bag or two?"

"Bottom drawer, left of the stove. Why?"

She opened the fridge. "It's a waste to leave all this food when you're not going to be here. Besides, it'll save me a trip to the grocery store."

"Right," he said, struggling to rise, the exertion giving his skin a rosy tint that complemented his tan. "Let me help you with that."

She waved him away. "I got it. Besides, not to be rude or anything, but you can't really carry much when your hands are handling crutches. Why don't you make sure you have everything you need and I'll load that ridiculously small space you call a trunk."

"It's a sports car, not a minivan. It's not made for hauling stuff," he said defensively as she headed past him with a loaded brown bag. "And try not to let anything spill back there."

"I'll give it my utmost attention," she said with a fake smile. With any luck the milk would topple and soak the damn thing.

## CHAPTER NINE

THE FOLLOWING DAY Nora took the steps to her father's home two at a time and went inside.

"Dad, I got something for you," she hollered, heading for the kitchen. "Ice-cold beer." She smiled as he appeared from his hobby room and checked down the hallway to make sure his other daughter wasn't around. "Coast is clear, Dad. Come and get some liquid refreshment."

Gerald accepted the beer from Nora and she put the rest of the six-pack into the fridge. She jerked her thumb. "Tell Nat if she throws these out, she's going to have to answer to me, 'cause they're mine. I don't know what she's thinking lately but it's annoying. I'm about ready to whack her over the head with a stick."

Gerald chuckled despite the promise of violence in Nora's comment and gestured they sit out on the porch where the sun was warm but not overly so.

Outside, Nora hopped onto the railing and settled against the support post while her father eased into the old swing. After a long, satisfying swallow of beer, he sighed and said, "Your sister means well. You shouldn't be so hard on her. She's got a full plate with those babies and now me. A daughter shouldn't have to shoulder so much."

Nora waved away his concern. "Nah, Nat is in her element. She wouldn't know what to do with herself if she wasn't mothering everyone. I just wish she'd lighten up a bit. I mean, what's the deal with her deciding what you can and can't eat or drink? She's your daughter, not your warden," she continued, affronted by the very idea. "It's not like you're an alcoholic or something."

Gerald sighed and took a slow slug. "Yeah, well, with your mom gone she's probably just trying to fill in the gaps. Missy used to get after me for having a beer or two. She'd complain and I'd bluster." He shrugged, a momentary sadness creeping into the warm air. "It was our thing, I guess."

"I never saw Mom argue with you," Nora countered with a soft snort. "When did this happen? Behind closed doors?"

Gerald slanted his gaze at her. "Maybe you didn't pay close enough attention to what was going on around you. Your mom got her point across without having to make a scene. It's a talent you didn't seem to inherit," he added.

"Hey! Who brought you beer?" she retorted, only slightly offended at his comment because it was true. He lifted his bottle in acknowledgment and her chuckle ended with a difficult realization. "I think I might've missed out on a lot with Mom. I spent way too much time fighting with her. There's a lot of things I never got to tell her."

"She knows."

"How do you know? You got a landline to heaven or something?" she joked. She then sighed and added, "If so, put her on speakerphone, I've got a few questions of my own."

He smiled. "I pity the man who decides to marry you. All piss and vinegar with only a sprinkle of sugar to make it all go down."

"Yeah, a spitting image of *you,* from what I hear," Nora said wryly. It felt good to banter; it'd been a long time since she'd felt the urge to do so. The easy silence between them allowed her mind to wander, and her thoughts went to Ben and his unusual circumstances. "Dad…" she began, feeling the need for a little parental advice but not entirely sure she wanted to hear it. "There was an accident and my client, Ben, got hurt. He's paying me to help him out, in addition to the landscaping job. We don't really get along that well but there's something about him that—" she shrugged in confusion "—I don't know, is interesting. There's something intriguing about him, I guess."

"You like him?"

She reacted with an immediate scoff. "Dad, I just said we don't get along. He's arrogant, snobby and completely at a loss without his Starbucks and art house theaters. He's the complete opposite of me. And he's irritating."

"So why are you helping him out?"

"Because it seemed like the right thing to do. He's all alone, his family is scattered and I guess I felt bad for him for a split second. Unfortunately my mouth reacted before my brain could stop it and I volunteered. And Doc Hessle didn't help either. He practically guilted me into taking the job. When's that man going to retire, for crying out loud?"

"You could've asked Rhonda's daughter, Kelly, to look after him for a while," he suggested, to which Nora scowled.

Kelly Crawston? A leggy redhead with fake boobs and an equally fake tan who was on the prowl for husband No. 2? "I said I don't like him, but I don't want to make his life miserable, Dad."

"Fair enough. But I'm sure there's plenty of people you could've rustled up to help the guy out."

"Well, I already offered, so it would be rude to back out now," she said. Plus, she hated the idea of some woman no doubt fawning over Ben once she caught a glimpse of those tightly muscled abs and devastating green eyes. If he managed to affect her in such a disturbing manner, what defenses could a single woman in Emmett's Mill possibly mount against the man? Given a chance, he could ruin every eligible female from here to Coldwater. In a way, Nora was sacrificing herself to protect the masses. Oh, whatever! *Sell that to someone who's buying.* Nora shut out the voice and realized her father was watching her speculatively.

"What?"

"Did I ever tell you how I met your mother?"

"No. Why?"

He swirled the remainder of his beer. "Let me tell you a story. I think you'll find it a good one."

"Dad, I don't want to hear how crazy you were over Mom. I already know that," she said plaintively, the idea of her parents being young and in love was nice, but learning any further details didn't appeal. She liked to think her parents had sex three times and that was the extent of it.

"Shut up and listen for once in your life," he growled, and she sighed, resigning herself to the story. "It was the summer of '66 and it was a hot, blistering son of a bitch. The grass was dry as tinder and the winds had finished off the low-lying shrubbery and trees. All it took to start a raging wildfire was one idiot tossing his lit cigarette out his car window and everything was ablaze for miles. At one point even Emmett's Mill was on the verge of evacuation.

"Well, I was on the CDF crew, working the summer like I'd been doing since I graduated from high school and was put on sandwich detail."

"Sandwich detail?" Nora arched her brow. Her big, brawny dad pulling the lunch wagon? "Who'd you piss off?"

"Doesn't much matter at this point," he countered with a mild glare, shifting his weight in the swing. "Suffice it to say it was me who went into Darlin's for the pickup."

"Darlin's?"

"Little sandwich shop that used to be

where the gym is now. Owned by Darlin Amensted before it changed a few hands and then finally closed down completely in the mid-1970s. Great place. Anyway, your mother happened to be working there for the summer and the minute I walked through that swinging door I—"

"Fell in love," Nora supplied in a half-bored voice.

"No, I thought she was the snippiest, snootiest, sassiest-mouthed thing I'd ever encountered."

Nora did a double take. "What?"

"See? You don't know so much after all. Now stop interrupting."

Chastised and more than a little surprised, she did exactly that. Mollified, Gerald began again, only as he spoke, his smile grew and Nora could feel the love he still felt as he told a story of two people who couldn't seem to stand each other at first blush.

"She had a temper to match my own, only hers was more dangerous because it was silent. Of course, I thought I was hot shit on a cold stick and was more than happy to show her who was boss, until I bit into my sandwich—how she knew it was mine, I'll never figure out—and instead of egg salad there were two thick slabs of pimento loaf and tons of mustard smeared all over it." He shuddered at the memory. "She got me good. I hate mustard, and pimento loaf ain't fit for criminals."

"You probably deserved it," Nora said, smiling at the picture in her head. "But I can't believe Mom did something like that. In my whole life I never heard her raise her voice to you. It used to drive me crazy."

"You don't know what she had to say in private. That woman could scald the insides of a person's ear without ever having to shout. She was quite a woman." He seemed lost in his reverie for a moment until his eyes cleared and he was back on track. "The point is, love hits us square in the forehead when we're not looking. Maybe you ought to give this Ben guy a second glance. Who knows? Maybe he's the only guy who can put up with your sass. God knows Missy knew how to handle my bluster."

Nora suppressed a shiver and sent her father a wry look. "Dad…I loved your story, but that's not how things are between me and Ben. It's my fault he's hurt. I hardly think that will make him want to marry me. Ugh. The very thought is disturbing."

Gerald chuckled. "Nora Marie, take it from someone who knows—you can run but you can't hide. If this man's under your skin, he's there for a reason. I guarantee it."

A FEW HOURS LATER Nora pulled into the driveway at Ben's and was puzzled to see another beat-up truck full of squawking, caged chickens and smelling like cow manure parked outside.

She grabbed the bag of supplies she'd bought at the hardware store and headed inside.

"Yes, I'm B.J.'s grandson but I'm only here temporarily, Mr.—"

"Buster's the name."

"Mr. Buster—"

"No, just Buster. I ain't one to stand on ceremony."

She set the bag in the kitchen and then moved toward the voices.

"Listen here, son. B.J. was a good man even though he was a lawyer. He and I worked out a deal for some work he did for my family and since he's not here I aim to fulfill my debt with you."

Ben saw Nora standing in the doorway and the look in his eyes begged for help.

The man identified as Buster turned and tipped his worn and dirty hat to Nora and then returned to Ben. "We's good folk and we honor our debt. So you and the missus here is gonna get fresh eggs delivered once a week and that's just how it is. Got a few chickens to spare, too. But seeing as you're just getting settled, we'll bring those later." He headed for the door and stopped short. "I was right sorry to hear of your grandparents passing the way they did. God must've needed himself two more angels up there but it's a right shame for us down here."

Ben struggled out of the faded armchair, trying to hop after the man but Buster was already outside. Nora pointed to the chair and indicated he put his butt back in it and went to the front door herself just in time to receive a pretty basket with a red gingham napkin folded over what she assumed were fresh eggs.

Buster gestured to the gingham. "That's the missus's idea. She likes to pretty things up. I'll be back next week same time, if it's all the same to you."

"Thanks, Buster. The eggs are great," she said, suppressing a giggle at the circumstances. "See you next week."

Buster waved and climbed into his truck, and once it rumbled down the driveway, she walked inside and returned to the living room where Ben sat with a confounded expression.

She set the basket on the end table and said, "Just so we're clear, I prefer cash—not eggs—as payment for services rendered."

"That makes two of us," he returned, raking a hand through his hair and leaving it ruffled and tantalizingly mussed.

Why'd he have to do that? Her good mood vanished, replaced with a need for something she couldn't put her finger on but needed badly enough to notice. She grabbed the eggs. "I'll put these in the fridge," she said, exhaling loudly. She wanted to regroup. She returned a few moments later with an interesting thought.

"You know, your grandfather used to work out of his home. I suspect you might have more people showing up on your doorstep once they find out you're here."

He looked horrified. "Why do you say that?"

She shrugged. "Just a guess, but judging by Buster's surprise visit I'd say if B.J. worked deals with anyone else, you might find yourself up to your elbows in bartered goods."

"You're not kidding, are you." His flat statement was rhetorical. "You've got to put a stop to this right now."

"Me?" Not on your life. "This is your problem. Not mine. You fix it."

"You know these people. You can finesse it."

She shot him a sardonic look. "I'm sorry. Have you met me? I don't finesse anything. Besides, just because I live here doesn't mean I know *everyone*. You're the lawyer. Talk your way out of it."

"You know, I'm getting tired of your insults. Can you say something without being rude or slanderous?"

She gave a show of thinking about it, then lifted her hands. "Nope. Seems not. And you're still in the same situation you were ten minutes ago. Fix it yourself, city boy."

"Fine, I will." He glared.

"Good." She grabbed the cordless phone and tossed it to him. "I've got a small backhoe coming in to tear up the old lawn and if there's an emergency you can call my cell."

"Wait a minute," he called out, causing her to pause and wait impatiently. "Did you leave me anything to eat? I'm paying you to take care of those types of details."

"Right." She pulled a candy bar from her back pocket and pitched it to him with a smarmy grin. "My favorite—Snickers. Enjoy."

BEN CAUGHT the candy bar and as his hand curled around it, he was tempted to hit Nora upside the head with it. He must've been out of his mind when he asked her to help him out. He'd liked to say it had sounded like a good idea at the time but that was a lie. He'd known it smacked of disaster. Well, he was paying for it now.

He ripped open the candy bar and devoured it in two bites. The chocolate hit a good spot and it tasted better than he'd anticipated. Perhaps it was the sugar high or the odd events of the morning that had thrown him off kilter, but he grabbed his crutches and hobbled his way carefully to the study area where his grandfather had apparently held court with the motley group he called clients.

His responsible nature demanded he focus on the Wallace case, but his curiosity effectively silenced that demand as he settled into the soft leather chair at the desk that seemed the only indulgence on his grandfather's part and started going through the piles of paperwork.

What he found created a bigger puzzle in his mind.

It was no wonder his grandparents were practically destitute when they died. Most of his grandfather's clients paid exactly in the manner Ben feared—the barter system.

Chickens. Heirloom tomato seeds. A purebred hound dog?

How'd they survive? And if the community was as poor as this—that the only way they could pay their bills was to bring odd items for trade—why did his grandparents stay?

Leaning back in the chair, he listened as it groaned softly with his weight and thought of the reasons his father had refused to let Ben visit his grandparents again the following summer.

His father had been reading the *Wall Street Journal* and had barely looked up when Ben had made his request. The answer had been a simple no.

"Why not?" he'd retorted, his young voice cracking with adolescent angst and hormonal change. "You let me go last year."

"That was your mother's idea."

"And?"

The paper dipped slightly to reveal his father's hard gaze. "And if it'd been up to me, you wouldn't have spent a moment with those people."

"They were nice," he said under his breath, but his father caught it.

"Nice?" he sneered. "What do you know about anything? You're just a kid. *Nice* people don't screw you out of your inheritance and claim it's for your own good."

"What inheritance?"

"What does it matter? It's gone. Given away to some nonprofit hospice for sick kids, but that was my money."

"How do you know it was yours?" Ben asked. "Maybe they didn't remember that they were going to give it to you."

"They knew. But since I'd already made my own fortune before that particular account matured, they said those sick kids needed it more. I had plans for that money and they didn't have the right. Stupid old geezers," his father muttered and returned to his paper.

Ben had sat stunned, unsure of what to say. He didn't like to hear his father talk of his parents like that and neither did he like seeing his father act so uncharitably toward those less fortunate. But his father was a hard and bitter man, and Ben had learned long ago not to try to change him. Dropping the subject, he never asked to visit his grandparents again.

Looking back, he realized he might've gone to his mother for answers, but Penny had been too busy securing her future with someone else to notice and even if she hadn't been distracted, she wasn't about to upset the gravy train with her ex-husband. Ben's father could be tightfisted when it pleased him and Penny had expensive tastes.

And, in all honesty, Ben had eventually lost interest in finding out the intricate details of what happened or even going to see the grandparents he'd known one summer. He sighed and let the paperwork drop to the desk and wondered what was going to show up on his doorstep next.

# *CHAPTER TEN*

SAMMY DROPPED down from the mini backhoe and accepted the bottled water from Nora, leaving a smear of mud where he wiped a bead of sweat from his dirt-speckled forehead.

"For April, it's damn hot out here," Sammy said after downing nearly half the bottle. "Well, you've been waiting to get your hands on this place for years. What are you going to do with it?"

"It's going to look gorgeous when I'm finished," Nora said with a huge grin. "I'm going to plant a few cedars over there as wind breakers and fresh grass all through here. A bower of English ivy creeping along an arched doorway to the herb garden—"

"Herb garden? Who'd you say your client was?" Sammy interrupted incredulously.

She scowled. "Stop being such a Neanderthal, Sammy. They're aromatic for one and useful for another. Remember when I used to make you that drink that soothed your stomach after a wild night of drinking? It was made from herbs, and I didn't hear you complaining. It was more like, 'Ooh, Nora, please make me some of that stuff, please!' That's how I remember it."

Sammy's ears reddened, but he didn't deny it. "Yeah well, that's you. You're a woman. I don't know of any *man* who grows a herb garden, so there."

"You should broaden your circle of acquaintances to include more than just beer buddies and bobble-headed bleached blondes with the IQ of a dish towel."

"Who pissed in your cornflakes today?" Sammy asked, only slightly ruffled by her comment. "You're not your usual sunny self."

A grin pulled at the corners of her mouth. She was never what anyone could call *sunny*. She shrugged, but her eyes strayed to the house and her thoughts went straight to Ben. She wasn't ready to share what was happening on that score—mostly because she didn't have a clue—and focused on something else. "So who's this Dana chick?"

Sammy faltered. "Dana…"

"Yeah, tall brunette paramedic who likes to pick fights with total strangers and make them feel like they've done something wrong when whatever happened was *clearly* an accident. Ring any bells?"

"Uh, she's new to town. Only been here about a year…"

"Yeah, I already got that much information. I'm interested in the part where my best friend was dating her and failed to mention this small detail."

Sammy looked away and hooked his thumbs on his jean pockets. "Aw, c'mon, Nora. Contrary to what you believe, I don't tell you everything in my personal life. Yeah, we were dating. And now we're not. Simple as that. Why? Where'd you see Dana?" he asked, staring keenly enough to destroy the nonchalance he was trying to project.

"She responded to Ben's accident."

"Ben? That's your client, right?"

"Yeah. He's inside. Fell down the ridge and nearly landed in the creek. He's pretty busted up. Anyway, she came and started acting like I pushed him or something."

"Did you?"

She shot him a dark look. "No."

"Just asking. You do have a temper. Need I remind you how I got this?" He pulled up his pant leg and revealed a faint scar that ran down his right shin.

"Someday you're going to need to find new material. I no longer feel guilty about that," she lied with great aplomb. "Besides, I told you not to jump. You're the one who had something to prove."

"You goaded me into jumping. I'm lucky to have limped away with a gash instead of a concussion."

She chewed the side of her cheek. Honestly, they had been fifteen and sixteen. A woman shouldn't have to pay for her mistakes her entire life. "It's not my fault you didn't clear the rock, and I hereby declare that incident inadmissible in future arguments."

"How so?"

"Ever hear of double jeopardy?" she asked.

He nodded warily, not quite sure where she was going with this. "Yeah, what of it?"

"I was punished pretty good for that little escapade down at the river. I'll have you know I spent the rest of my summer cleaning toilets up at my dad's CDF station, and let me tell you that was punishment enough."

Sammy burst into laughter. "You're right—you've paid your due. I promise not to use that one anymore. I've got plenty of others."

Of that she didn't doubt. As often as Sammy had been her partner in crime, he'd also been her guinea pig on numerous adventures. It was a miracle they were both still alive.

They sobered and Sammy started clearing his gear. "I'll be back tomorrow around 9:00 a.m. to start tearing up the side yard. I've got something to do or else I'd finish it now."

"Yeah? Hot date?"

He grinned but it was pained around the edges. "Not really. Just need to clear something up."

"Does this have anything to do with that paramedic?"

"She has a name."

"Touchy. All right, does this have anything to do with *Dana?*"

"Maybe."

Nora eyed Sammy. This tight-lipped routine wasn't like him. She accepted the empty water bottle, but she wasn't finished with the conversation. She didn't like being on the outside—yet another reason she didn't care for this interloper. She wanted her Sammy back. "You want to go get a beer after your thing?"

"Uh, aren't you busy with Ben?"

Yes. Damn. She shrugged. "He's not

paying me to be his beck-and-call girl. I'll leave him with a bowl of water and some kibble."

Sammy grinned knowingly as he climbed into his truck. "Knowing you and your cooking skills, it most likely will be kibble. I pity the poor guy. He doesn't know what he's taken on."

That was true in more ways than one. Nora would rather spend an evening listening to Sammy whine about his lost love than spend an evening alone with Ben. He made her feel uneasy. Not to mention ravenous for his naked flesh. She patted the beads of sweat from her forehead and chased after Sammy. "You sure? Hanging out with that guy makes me crazy. I can only take his attitude for so long. C'mon... me, you, a couple of rounds at Gilly's? First round's on me."

He waved her away and gunned the engine. "Rain check. I gotta take care of this and I don't know how long it'll take. See you tomorrow."

Fine. "Traitor," she mumbled, and turned on her heel and faced the house. Ben was inside, working like a busy, overworked robot bee—probably oblivious to the effect he had on her—and she was standing outside like a ninny when she ought to just tell him he'll have to find someone else to be his nurse. She trudged inside and put on a stoic—completely unaffected—face for an audience of one.

BEN WAS STILL SITTING in his grandfather's office, knee-deep in paperwork when Nora came in at the end of the day.

"Ben?"

"In the study," he called out.

She appeared in the doorway. "What are you doing?" she asked, sounding a little alarmed at the piles of paperwork he'd spent all day separating into some semblance of order. "Isn't it illegal to go through someone's things?"

"Not when the owner is dead and the person who's going through those things inherited the estate. Have a seat. I have some questions you might be able to answer."

"Yes, Counselor?" she said, sinking into a nearby chair with an amused expression. "What can I do for you?"

"Thanks to our egg-paying friend Buster and your earlier comment, I got to thinking I better find out exactly how many clients bartered for service. Honestly, I thought it would be easy, seeing as the town's not so big, and well, how many eggs could one man possibly need?" He sighed. "But it goes beyond eggs."

"Beyond eggs? Like bartered milk? Or completely out of the dairy family?"

"I'm serious."

"Did everyone lose their sense of humor today?" she mumbled, but gave him her full attention. "What are you saying?"

"B.J. and Corrinda bartered for eighty percent of their income. From homemade casseroles to bushels of fresh apples. In this day and age, I just can't wrap my brain around the fact that they managed to turn back time and live as frugally as possible with very little money."

"That would explain why the house started to look so ramshackle."

"Yeah, apparently B.J. hadn't done any work for a carpenter or gardener before they died," he said with a healthy dose of sarcasm.

"Hey, watch it. I liked them—a lot—remember? And I for one think it's kinda cool. Very old world."

"It's not cool," he retorted, astounded at her opinion. "It's…it's ridiculous. And do these people expect me to reciprocate because my addled grandfather chose to?"

"Maybe until they meet you. One face-to-face meeting with you will probably clear up any misconceptions they might have."

"Yeah, well, I didn't have much luck in dissuading Buster, now, did I?" He pushed a hand through his hair. "What kind of hillbilly hell has my crazy old coot of a grandfather gotten me into?"

"I said watch it," she murmured low in her throat. "He wasn't addled or crazy. He was kind and generous and clearly cared about his clients. He believed everyone should have legal representation, no matter their financial situation."

"Yeah, so does the Constitution, which provides legal counsel for those who can't afford their own."

"It provides for people charged with a *crime*. It doesn't say anything about a seventy-year-old rancher facing off with the state when they threatened to withdraw the Williamson Act contract on his land, which would have tripled his property taxes and basically forced him to declare bankruptcy and move."

He stared at her sudden vehemence. "You're saying my grandfather helped someone like that?"

"Yes, that's what I'm saying," she snapped.

"Then where's the documentation?" he

demanded, shaking a sheaf of paperwork. "Everything else is here. Hell, here's a paper for the barter of a purebred hound dog, which as far as I can tell, didn't come with the house. I don't care to inherit a flea-bitten mutt as well as all this junk."

Nora shot to her feet, her eyes flashing. "His name is George Brummel. He owns hundreds of acres off Highway 140. The property's been in his family for generations, and the Williamson Act contract enabled them to keep the land as long as it was designated agricultural or kept as open space. The Brummel family was once a proud, flourishing group of people who helped build Emmett's Mill. In fact, Hop Brummel—George's great-great-grandfather—has his name scratched into the mortar of one of the oldest buildings in town, built in the 1800s. George came to B.J. for help, and B.J. saved the Brummel legacy. I don't see anything *ridiculous* about that." She was almost out the door when she reconsidered and left one final comment. "As for the dog, his name was Howie the Howler, and you don't have to worry about him because he died of heartworm complications a few months before B.J. and Corrinda. And they were devastated, you prick!"

A door slammed and rattled every window

in the house and Ben knew Nora was gone. Grimacing, he grabbed his crutches and hobbled from the room, an unsettled feeling in his gut to match the echo of Nora's parting comment. He *was* a prick and he wished to God he didn't come by it so naturally, but it flowed through his veins as surely as his own blood.

Perhaps it was better this way. At least Nora wouldn't mistake him for anything else.

# CHAPTER ELEVEN

NORA RETURNED the following day and waved to the crew she'd hired to start preparing the ground for planting, before reluctantly heading inside. She shouldn't have left the way she did but Ben managed to push every button she had and her temper flared before she had a chance to launch a defense. Her mom had been fond of telling her to act like an adult, so in deference to that advice, Nora came with a peace offering of sorts.

"Ben?" she called out, knowing better this time than to barge into his bedroom for fear of sending her hormones into overdrive again. She hollered again. "Are you decent? I have something for you."

There was swearing coupled with a loud bang in the kitchen and Nora jumped before rushing to investigate.

"What are you doing? Remodeling the kitchen?" she asked, rounding the corner to find Ben standing over a skillet with what looked like some type of omelet on the tile floor. She clapped a hand over her mouth to keep from giggling at Ben's frustrated expression at the demise of what she assumed was going to be a delicious breakfast. "What was it?"

"Denver omelet," Ben said from between pressed lips. "It's very hard to balance on crutches and carry a hot skillet."

Nora grabbed a few paper towels and began mopping up the mess. "Don't you think that was a little ambitious for a man in your condition?" she asked, dumping the soiled towels in the wastebasket and surveying the remains of red and green peppers, onion and fresh chives on the cutting board.

"Yes, but I wanted to do something to make amends for my behavior yesterday," he said, looking more miserable by the moment. "You were right. I was being a prick. I figured the one thing I could do was make you a nice breakfast but it seems I can't even do that right now."

"Well, good thing Buster is bringing more eggs next week. Looks like most of them are on the floor," she said, biting back a smile. It was incredibly sweet. She'd have to be made of stone not to appreciate the effort. Why he cared what she thought was baffling but it gave her a dark thrill just the same. "It's funny, because I brought you something for breakfast, although it's nothing like you were trying to whip up." She opened the small grocery bag and pulled out two muffins the size of a plate and two short coffees.

"We don't have a Starbucks, but we do have a coffee joint that's pretty close. You don't seem the type to drink fancy sugared drinks so I went with black. Is that all right?"

His face lost some of its frustration and a smile smoothed out the tension in his lips. "Perfect," he said, accepting both the coffee and a muffin.

"Seems we're both sorry for yesterday," Nora began as she peeled the wrapper from her muffin. "It's no excuse but it bothers me when you talk like that about your grandparents. I wish you could've known them better. They were good people."

"Nora, I'm not doubting they were good people…but you have to admit, my grandfather went a little overboard with the bartering. I mean, look at the house. It was practically falling down around their ears. I think that's irresponsible."

"Maybe they were trying to create a world that was more equal than the one we live in."

"There's no such thing as a utopia.

Everyone has needs and my grandparents needed cold hard cash."

Nora set her muffin down. "I can see that. Why didn't your parents kick down some or, for that matter, why not you? Judging by that car, you have some to spare."

He fell silent, uncomfortable with the turn in the conversation. She didn't blame him. One wrong word and they'd end up fighting again. He drew a deep breath before continuing. "I didn't know they needed money," he said carefully. "If I'd known…well, I'd have helped as much as I could, though I should level with you, the car's not mine."

"Whose is it?"

"My dad's."

She stared but her mouth trembled with the effort not to burst out laughing. "You're telling me, at thirty-four years old you're still driving around in daddy's car?"

He scowled. "For practical reasons. I can afford to buy my own, but he rarely drives the vehicle and I don't see the logic in just letting it sit in a garage. Besides, my dad rarely visits the West Coast, so it's practically mine."

"I see." *Spoken like a true spoiled brat.* She shook her head and popped a piece of muffin in her mouth. "So what's the deal with your parents, then? Why didn't they offer to help your grandparents?"

"It seems they had a falling-out before I was born and it was never resolved," Ben said, shifting on his crutches. "And before you ask, no, I don't know exactly what happened between them, but it had something to do with money and an inheritance my father believed belonged to him."

"If that's the case, that would explain why your grandfather eschewed money for trade. Money was responsible for ruining his family."

Ben appeared thoughtful. "Yes, I suppose that's one way of looking at it."

"Do you have another theory?" Nora asked.

"Nora, I can't possibly offer any kind of educated guess or theory without all the facts. I'd have to ask my father for his view of the situation to get an idea and without my grandfather's version, it would only be one-sided."

"Still, it'd be something. I don't understand how you can live your life in complete ignorance of something so big in your family."

"There's the difference between you and me. It doesn't affect my life, so therefore I don't care to know."

Nora snorted softly. "How do you know it doesn't affect your life? Ben…if things had been different in your life, don't you think you might have sustained a relationship with your grandparents? That maybe you might have known them for more than one summer?"

Ben's demeanor changed. A long pause punctuated their conversation until he drew himself up and forced a tight smile. "Nora, it doesn't matter what I think, it won't change what happened. I grew up without them. That's how it goes. Thanks for the muffin and coffee. If you don't mind, I'm going to drag myself into the shower."

*So much for making amends,* Nora thought grimly.

LATER THAT DAY, head throbbing and stomach queasy from the pain medication, Ben decided to take a break from the Wallace case and found himself watching Nora from the study window.

The day couldn't have been more glorious; the blue sky gave no hint of the storm that was supposed to be coming tonight, and Nora was completely in her element—which appeared to be knee deep in dirt. Although she'd hired a small crew to tear apart the yard, she didn't slough off the tough jobs. Earlier, when his focus had wandered and fastened on Nora she was manhandling a ro-totiller with the ease of a seasoned laborer. Her small frame was muscled and when she'd stood to stretch her back, Ben had caught a glimpse of her near-perfect belly as her shirt had risen, teasing him with a land-scape he'd never travel.

A grudging smile tugged at his lips, safe in the knowledge no one was apt to catch the unguarded moment. His gaze went to the strong line of her calf, bare to the sun thanks to an old pair of cut-off jeans that were nearly indecent the way they hugged her behind and set his imagination on fire. She was like Daisy Duke, Princess Leia and every other boyhood fantasy all wrapped up in one sassy package that was so out of his reach he'd get a cramp if he tried.

Ben didn't suffer from an inferiority complex, he just knew his limitations. He didn't have the time to deal with the compli-cations that would come with dating someone like Nora. Logical advice. But, as he watched her high blond ponytail bounce as playfully as a child on a playground, he couldn't help but wonder what those golden strands would feel like sliding through his fingers, or better yet, brushing across his face. His hardening groin jolted him out of his idle thoughts and forced him to return to the Wallace case and all it entailed.

Even as he stared at property lists and income declarations, his mind refused to stay on track, inching again toward forbidden territory as he pondered why someone with so much to offer was still single. Her temper was surely a mark on the not-so-desirable list, he thought with a wince as his side twinged. But he'd never met anyone with such an abundance of spirit. And so beautiful, sometimes it made his teeth ache from wanting. He heard her laughter—robust and full, no hesitation—and returned to the window, wanting to know who had made her laugh so easily.

The brawny guy running the backhoe grabbed her by the neck, looking as if he was burying her in his armpit, until she twisted out of his grip and whacked him in the butt with the top of her tennis shoe. Even from a distance, Ben could sense a bond between the pair that left him struggling with the impulse to separate them. A ridiculous thought at best, he scoffed, deliberately moving away from the window. It didn't matter how she felt about him nor that she'd never shared a bit of genuine laughter with him. Scooping the files he needed, he hobbled from the room, not to escape the sound of her laughter, but to keep himself from caring.

NORA ENDED THE DAY tired but pleased with the progress they were making. The yard looked like hell—giant furrows of freshly churned soil exposed thick roots of old trees that Nora wanted to save, and the air was thick with the smell of earth, water and crushed grass, but the promise of what could be filled her with barely bridled excitement. Nora drew a deep, restorative breath, savoring the smell assaulting her senses, and wondered if anyone else enjoyed gardening as much as she did. She loved her job.

Twisting sharply to ease the kinks in her back, she smiled as a chorus of pops and snaps sounded from her spine. *Ahhh...that felt good*.

Now for her second job. She gave herself a quick mental pep talk filled with advice on how much easier life would be if she minded her own business and stopped wondering if he was a boxer or briefs kind of guy and walked into the house.

Aside from the soft ticktocking of the multitude of clocks, the house was silent. She found Ben, as she expected to, bent over his grandfather's desk, his brow furrowed, one finger pressed against his lips while he perused a sheaf of papers. She knocked on the door frame and was privately delighted by the way his eyes lit up momentarily.

"Finished for the day. I was fixin' to head out. Do you need anything before I go?"

A hungry light flared in his eyes that took her breath away but he shook his head and returned to his reading.

Wait a minute. She pursed her lips, knowing what she'd seen hadn't been a mirage. What's behind door No. 2? "I have an idea," she said, brooking his attention once more. "Let's get out of here for the night."

He blinked. "Excuse me?"

"You know, blow off some steam, get a bite to eat or just, um, I don't know, just change the scenery a bit. You look like you could use a break from whatever it is you're doing."

He chuckled in a way that told her he wasn't about to take her up on her offer and said, "Thanks, but I have more work than I can possibly handle and it wouldn't be prudent to stop."

"C'mon, Ben. Where's your sense of adventure? You need to loosen up, live a little. What's an hour or two? Surely you can swing that."

He opened his mouth to—no doubt—politely but firmly decline, but he must've sensed that she wasn't going to back down and in the interest of his sanity, agreed. "An hour? I suppose I can."

Nora clapped her hands in victory. "Great! What'll it be? Gilly's or the Grill? You feel like bad pizza, beer and peanuts or an overpriced hamburger that'll make you wonder if Reggie stole the recipe from some four-star place." She eyed him speculatively. "Actually, you don't seem like the beer-and-peanuts kind of guy. How about the Grill?"

"I like beer and pizza," he retorted, mildly offended. "Just because I don't wear flannel and tote a wrench on my belt doesn't mean I can't appreciate the simpler elements of life."

"Right. Say something like that to anyone else and you might get your butt kicked. The Grill, it is. Grab your coat. My truck is drafty, as you may remember."

He stopped short after settling his crutches under his arm, a look of distaste on his fine features. "Let's take my car."

"Are you kidding me? My dad is a card-carrying member of the I Only Buy American Made club. If I drive into town in that fancy import I'm likely to be lynched—or at the very least disowned—by my family. No thanks. Button up. It's Bettina or bust."

She left the room with Ben following close behind. When they were at the front door, she turned to find him looking at her curiously. "What?"

"Am I to believe you actually named your truck?"

"Damn straight. Cars have personality whether you believe it or not. My dad had a '73 'Cuda that I swear was a cousin to Stephen King's Christine. She only let my dad drive her." She stifled a giggle. "My sister Natalie actually stalled her when she was sixteen and learning to drive. It was an automatic!"

"How do you stall an automatic?" he asked, grabbing his coat from the hall tree as they closed the door behind them.

Nora grinned. "I have no idea. You'd have to ask Natalie. But a word of advice if you do…be prepared to duck. She's had about twenty years of our teasing. She probably won't take too kindly to you joining in!"

"If her temper is anything like yours, I won't mention it at all," he said dryly.

Nora flashed him a teasing smile. "It appears that Ivy-League education was good for something."

He laughed and climbed into the truck, hanging his elbow casually out the window like any country boy might on an evening ride, and Nora had to stop herself from picturing him in other aspects of her life. They were from two different worlds. Sure, she was college-educated as well, but Ben wore his education like a shield, whereas Nora preferred to keep things simple and only dusted off her Cal Poly University education when needed.

They arrived at the Grill and Nora rumbled into a tight parking spot with ease, laughing at Ben's apprehension. "I've been parking Bettina in smaller places than this for years. And you should see me parallel park," she added with a confident wink before climbing out of the truck.

A smile borne of grudging admiration tilted his mouth, and Ben followed her slowly as they entered the bustling restaurant.

NORA LED BEN to a spot away from the lounge entrance where country music blared and bodies could be glimpsed shaking and grooving despite the early-evening hour. He relaxed into the chair, glad to get off the crutches for a minute. His underarms were sore from the pressure and his back felt out of whack from sitting with his foot elevated for most of the day.

"So what's good here?" Ben asked over the crowded scene.

"Everything," Nora answered smugly just as their waitress came over to them wearing big hoop earrings and a wide-mouthed grin painted with fire-engine-red lipstick.

"Who's your friend?" the waitress gestured, flashing that clown smile Ben's way. There was no mistaking her flirtatious intention. "I haven't seen you around, so you must be from out of town. I know everyone."

"Ben meet Jenny, the local 411 directory," Nora said in dry introduction.

"Nice to meet you, Jenny," Ben said politely, accepting a menu. "And, no, I'm not from around here."

"Yep, thought so. I'm pretty good with faces…and other things. What happened to your foot?" Jenny asked with sympathy.

Ben shot a look at Nora and she blushed but all he did was shrug and answer, "Wasn't watching where I was going and tripped."

"Aw, you poor thing. Need any help with anything? Anything at all?"

Nora snapped her fingers at Jenny before Ben could respond to her blatant innuendo and he was immensely grateful until she started giving the poor girl a ration. "Yo, Jenny, keep your eyes in your head and your hands to yourself. Besides, I know you're dating Timmy Landers, so don't go eyeing candy you'll never get to taste."

Ben caught his mouth before it dropped open, but Jenny retorted with only a slight pout saying, "Don't get yourself in a twist. I was just kidding. Anyway, you know I like 'em country." She sent Ben a playful look that was only slightly less lascivious than the first. "But I don't mind looking at the city lights once in a while."

"I'm flattered...I think," he added, wondering if Nora hadn't been sitting across from him if Jenny might've added him to the menu for the night. He caught Nora's narrowed gaze before she returned to her menu with a muttered expletive and ordered buffalo wings and two beers to start.

"You got it," Jenny said, throwing a wink over her shoulder for Ben's benefit.

"Was that good for your ego?" Nora asked after Jenny was out of earshot, smiling too sweetly to be trusted.

Ben chuckled with a shrug. Maybe if the

woman wasn't completely off the charts from his type, but he withheld his answer, choosing to let Nora draw her own conclusion. "She seems like a nice woman."

Nora snorted. "She's nice to everyone. And when I say everyone—"

"I get it," he cut in wryly.

Her smile turned devilish. "You're a smart man."

"Thanks. Glad to hear my education hasn't gone to waste. I take it you and she aren't the best of friends?"

"Why would you say that?"

He arched his brow. "Because most people don't insinuate their friends are loose women."

"What if it's the truth? I'm not saying anything Jenny wouldn't tell you herself. I'm just saving you the trouble of finding out the hard way."

"Thanks," he said, his voice warming with the laughter he felt bubbling inside. If he didn't know better, he'd say Nora was a little jealous. Odd, given their circumstances, but he didn't deny enjoying the possibility. "I appreciate your looking out for my well-being. If you're ever in the Bay Area in the social scene frequented by attorneys and their clients, I'll be sure to point out the ones to avoid."

Like Ed Wallace, his thoughts immediately going to the paunchy older man who was, at this minute, probably engaging in all sorts of debauchery because he could pay for people's discretion.

"You know a few bad apples, huh?"

"A few."

"How bad?"

He met her gaze. "Bad enough."

Jenny arrived with their hot wings and beer and after taking their order for the main course, disappeared again without so much as batting an eyelash this time around.

Nora grabbed a wing and within seconds had sucked the meat from the bone. Her lips, wet and glossy from the hot sauce that Ben could tell the moment it hit his taste buds could probably sear the enamel off his teeth, began to swell slightly from the heat. It was all Ben could do not to choke or stare like a man who hadn't been with a woman in over a year.

He matched Nora and grabbed another wing, noting that she didn't once reach for her beer even though *he* was dying to cool the inferno in his mouth. If she could take it, so could he. An alarm sounded in his brain and his eyes watered but he reached for another, smiling through his tears as if he could do this all night.

"So tell me about these bad guys you

know," Nora said, wiping the corner of her mouth with her napkin before digging into another wing and almost making Ben's eyes cross at doing the same but he did it anyway. "Just how bad are we talking? I thought you practiced only family law. I mean, it's not like you're representing murderers or anything."

He swallowed with difficulty. Had she no taste buds? This was insane. He eyed the tall draft and his mouth watered in time with the flow threatening to spill from his eyes. No. He wouldn't drink until she did. He focused on answering her question. "You'd be surprised by some of the despicable things people will do to one another in the throes of a custody battle or property dispute. One woman actually accused her husband of molesting their daughter when that wasn't even the case, but the girl—who was only five at the time—had to undergo a sexual-assault examination, which later traumatized the poor kid more so than the divorce of her parents. In the end, we found out the woman had only said that to try to keep the man from his daughter."

Nora stopped eating for a moment and the clearly disturbed expression on her face mirrored what he'd felt that day. "Let me guess…you were the woman's attorney?"

"You guessed it."

"So when it came out that he hadn't done anything to his daughter, what happened then?"

"The father got full custody and the woman was required to serve community service for perjuring herself."

"Seems kinda light for lying on the witness stand," Nora balked. "And about something so awful. I guess you can't control that part. Either way, justice was served, right? Must've felt good to see someone who deserved to win actually take home the prize."

He attempted a smile, but honestly, at this point, he couldn't feel his lips any longer and the gesture wouldn't have been genuine anyway. Losing that case had felt morally satisfying but had jeopardized his job. Layla Griggs's family had deep pockets and had paid Ben's firm handsomely to assure a win. When they hadn't…well, it wasn't pretty. "Yeah, it did."

Nora reached for her beer, and Ben nearly wept with relief on the inside but waited a whole half second before picking up his own. He crowed at this small victory until Nora gave him a wide grin, saying, "Not bad for a beginner. I was wondering how long you'd hold out."

"It wasn't that bad," he lied.

"Really? 'Cuz that's the mild sauce. We could call for a plate of the real hot stuff if you want," she teased.

"God, no!" Ben exclaimed, not knowing whether Nora was bluffing and not willing to chance it. "You win. My taste buds can't take another round of that stuff."

As she laughed and reveled in her victory, they fell into the kind of comfortable conversation that Ben realized he hadn't enjoyed in a long time. It seemed most of his social interactions of late had been client related and he never felt content to be himself in those situations. And since his last girlfriend, Olivia, left, he hadn't felt the urge to do anything beyond casual dating.

Ben studied Nora's animated expression as she spoke, watching as her gray eyes lit up with unabashed excitement as she launched into another story that Ben had lost the thread to long ago. He was more captivated by how beautiful she was and wondering why someone hadn't slapped a ring on her finger by now.

*What the hell are you thinking?* his brain whispered harshly, reminding him that inviting more intimate interaction was asking for trouble and further complications to a relationship that was already rife with them. *Don't ask about her personal life. It's none of your business.* Sound advice if he ever heard any—too bad the temptation was too great to listen.

"So how'd you manage to get through your early twenties without getting snagged by one of the locals?" he asked casually, grabbing her attention and dimming the light in her eyes. Her reaction immediately piqued his interest even as he sensed it was a subject she didn't want to talk about.

"I never felt the urge to settle down. You?"

"Same." He washed the remainder of the hot sauce from his mouth with a swallow of beer, watching and waiting to see if she would elaborate. She didn't. Instead she turned the spotlight back on him.

"I find it hard to believe a guy like you has remained single his entire adult life. You never met anyone special?"

"I didn't say that," he equivocated. Olivia had been special but not enough in her estimation. "I've had a number of serious relationships. Your turn."

She chuckled, but the sound wasn't as light and airy as it could have been. "Let's just say I haven't had the best of luck in that department."

"How so?"

A wry look followed. "How do you think? I've managed to hook up with all the wrong guys. The last one was married." At his startled expression, she clarified, "I didn't know he was married until his wife showed up at their lakeside cabin and caught us in a compromising position."

"Ouch. Surprised you managed to get out of there alive."

"You and me both. I didn't blame her, though. Her husband duped us both. I think they're divorced now."

"And he didn't come slinking back once he didn't have his wife anymore?"

She crooked a sardonic brow. "He did, but I think I communicated my thoughts quite succinctly when I leveled a shotgun at his cheating ass. He never came around again."

He grinned at the image of a gun-toting Nora and didn't envy the poor sap who'd underestimated his bed partner. "Do you have a license for that firearm?" he asked half-seriously.

"Of course. I've been registered to own a gun since I was eighteen. I'm a better shot than most of the guys down at the shooting range. You shoot?"

He shook his head. "No, but I can swing a mean 10-iron."

"Of course, what was I thinking? You're a lawyer, for crying out loud. Your idea of adventure is probably heading over to the bad side of town to grab a scotch."

"Hey, now you're getting mean. For your information, I can handle a bow and arrow pretty well. I used to belong to an archery club."

"Impressive...sort of." She laughed, the light slowly returning to her eyes as she relaxed. The conversation returned to safer topics and over the course of dinner, Ben realized he didn't want the evening to end. She was a lively dinner companion—funny, smart, articulate, despite her propensity for playing up her country roots, and damn attractive. How was he going to keep a professional distance when all he could think of was pulling her into his arms and tasting those lips and watching those expressive eyes go dewy and soft while her body melted into his?

As his grandmother might've said if he'd gotten to know her better...he was in a real pickle.

## CHAPTER TWELVE

NORA WAS OUTSIDE Ben's house, fertilizing the soil in preparation for the rows of flowers she'd picked to rim the side yard, when Sammy tore into the driveway, kicking up dust and gravel, angry music blaring. She straightened with a frown. *What's got him all bent?*

He stalked past her and went straight to the mini backhoe, and before she could get a word in, he gunned the engine and it roared to life.

"Careful! You break it, you buy it," she yelled over the noise, reminding Sammy that he was abusing a rental with her name on the signature line.

Sammy gave a curt nod to indicate he'd heard and gentled his actions but didn't respond otherwise. Guess he wasn't up to talking about whatever was eating him. Nora wasn't worried; Sammy would spill sooner or later. Besides, Nora had other things to occupy her mind.

She hoisted another bag of fertilizer and shook it out, the pungent odor assaulting her nostrils and prompting a grimace. Perhaps if she worked herself to exhaustion each day until the job was finished she wouldn't be thinking of things she had no business thinking. Like Ben.

She groaned and grabbed a hoe to spread the odiferous mix. While she may have invited him out to dinner for humanitarian reasons—the guy needed to get out of the house before he went stir-crazy—the end result had been disturbing. For a short time, she caught a glimpse of a different version of Ben, one that laughed easily, had a dry sense of humor that she completely appreciated since it mirrored her own, and when he flashed a playful smile at her, her insides had done silly flips and flutters and she'd hungered for something far less tangible than the food on her plate.

Plain and simple…she was wildly attracted to him and keeping her hands to herself wasn't as appealing an idea as it had been before.

The final layer of fertilizer finished, she headed into the house to scrub her hands.

A quick wash later, she told herself to go right back to work, but her feet didn't listen, and she headed straight for Ben's study.

He saw her coming and for a split second his eyes lit up and that blink of time sent her to cloud nine until she realized she was grinning from ear to ear and probably looked like a lovesick puppy.

"Need anything?"

He studied her as if contemplating something, then slowly nodded. "Actually, I do."

"Thirsty? Hungry? What do you need?"

"A date."

The air escaped her lungs in a whoosh and she stiffened. "I doubt Jenny is available. She's dating someone. A big, burly dumb ox of a guy who'd be likely to tear your arms off and beat you with them if you came near his girl. Sorry."

He startled her with a gusty laugh. "Thanks for the warning, but no, I wasn't looking for a date with Jenny. I was hoping you were available."

Her cheeks warmed. "Me?" Geez, was that her voice that sounded so high-pitched? She cleared her throat and tried again, this time shooting for a pleasantly curious tone. "Why me?"

"Well, it seems to make the most sense. I have a business engagement in the city that I can't get out of and since I already bought the tickets and I need you to drive…it's the most practical solution."

*Oh.* Her hopes deflated with a hiss. Of course it was practical. His car only sat two—didn't leave much room for a chauffeur and a real date. "I'll check my schedule," she retorted, suddenly intensely aware of how filthy—and smelly—she was at that moment. "When is this business thing?"

"Tomorrow."

She looked at him in annoyance. "Tomorrow? That's a little late notice don't you think?"

"Yes, I'm sorry. I tried to get out of it, but there are certain events at my firm that require attendance. The Poppenshier Benefit is one of them.

"Poppenshier?"

"Weird name, good cause. It's a benefit for a high-profile children's center for abused youth. My firm is a major benefactor. We give a substantial gift every year and my boss likes his top attorneys there."

"And you're one of them," she surmised.

He nodded without a hint of modesty, and she couldn't help but bristle just a little. "Well, I don't know if I'm free tomorrow. You might have to find yourself someone else." She turned, intending to leave before her bruised feelings became too evident, but the sound of his voice stopped her.

"Nora...I would really like you to come with me."

"Because it's convenient."

"Because...I enjoy your company. You're not like most women and, despite your eccentricities, I find you fascinating."

She thawed just a little. "What kind of dress requirement is there for this shindig?"

"Black-tie. Do you have anything you can wear on such short notice?"

She pictured Ben in a sharp black tux and her heartbeat sped up. In answer, she nodded. "Do you have anything against red?"

His gaze sharpened and roamed her body in a hungry perusal that she felt down to her toes. He slowly shook his head. "Red sounds fine by me. Be here by four? The dinner starts at six and we don't want to hit traffic."

She noted the mundane details, but a part of her brain was still focused on the feral look Ben had given her, as if he'd somehow seen into her closet to the hot red number that clung to her curves and breasts and the pair of sassy heels that helped add height to her slight frame.

"All right, it's a date," she finished, swallowing hard as she practically flew from the room, not quite sure why she was agreeing to such madness, but reveling in the adventure and hoping it didn't end as some adventures do…with a crash and burn.

BEN SPENT most of the afternoon fighting his baser, more primal nature and tried to focus on work rather than his uncomfortably tight groin area. He adjusted himself in annoyance, feeling much like a randy teenager who couldn't control his anatomy. But one thought of Nora on his arm, dressed to the nines, sent his pulse racing and his mind moving in R-rated directions. Did she feel the same? Did she wonder what she'd feel like pressed against him? Tongues dancing together, moving in a slick tango that sent heat spiraling through their bodies until clothes were an abomination and had to be discarded before they both went up in flames? He shuddered and scrubbed his hands down his face, wondering if he'd just made a huge mistake by inviting Nora deeper into his life.

He supposed he'd find out soon enough.

THE NEXT DAY Nora stood before Ben's front door, her insides shaking and fingers tingling as she tried to relax. This was a dinner engagement, a social function, that's all. No sense in making a huge deal out of something that had all the potential to be a big fat nothing.

So why was she so hesitant to open that door?

Nora pushed the thought out of her head and propelled herself inside, gritting her teeth against the spiraling sensation in her gut that felt too much like excitement.

Ben was standing in the foyer waiting, and despite the crutches, he looked every bit the stylish sophisticate with a polished air reminiscent of Pierce Brosnan in the *Thomas Crown Affair*. In a word: ohhhhhhh…

But even as she was ogling him shamelessly, he was doing the same.

"Beautiful," he murmured finally, warming her insides, as he did a slow perusal.

"An improvement from the usual Levi's and dirt," she said, fighting the urge to bite her lip.

"I'd say," he said, his voice drifting over her bare shoulders in a soft caress. The moment was fraught with tension that Nora knew to be dangerous, but the delicious feeling was alluring. The scrutiny in his gaze cleared and the corner of his mouth lifted in a subtle smile as he gestured toward the door. "Shall we, then?"

Moment broken, Nora lifted her chin and

met his smile with a sassy one of her own. "Yeah, let's get this show on the road. I don't want to spend all night around a bunch of lawyers."

She turned and gave him a nice view of her backside, knowing the smooth lines of the dress looked fabulous, and made her way to the car.

*You can look, but you can't touch.* She grinned from ear to ear. Tonight she was going to make Benjamin Hollister's eyes cross.

Guaranteed.

THEY ARRIVED on time despite a traffic snarl on the 880 and when they finally entered the glittering building and moved past the woman guarding the entrance, ensuring only those with an invitation gained entry, Nora was struck by the glamour of the backdrop.

"Pretty swanky place," Nora murmured, taking in the glitzy ballroom with the crystal chandeliers and rich burgundy wall hangings rippling in the subtle bay breeze coming from the open doors. "How many times have you been to this benefit dinner?"

He shrugged. "Since my first year at the firm."

"So what can I expect tonight?"

He shifted on his crutches and grimaced as he repositioned his weight. "Well, first there's an interminable amount of mixing with the overprivileged members of San Francisco society coupled with copious amounts of alcohol to make the experience remotely palatable. Then there's the overpriced dinner of something fancy and unrecognizable, and when everyone is good and drunk, there's a live auction for items that are—"

"Overpriced," Nora interjected with a smile.

He grinned. "You get the idea. But, as I mentioned, it's all for a good cause."

She scanned the room, taking careful note of those milling around, and surmised, "These are your friends?"

"Friends? No, I wouldn't say that."

"Then what would you say?"

"I'd say some are people I work with, others are clients and the rest are unknowns."

She chuckled. "Unknowns? Sounds like a math equation."

"It's all about networking. The only reason I come to this function is because my boss asks me to and the reason he asks is so that our firm has a presence among the elite who, by the way, are always just one step shy of needing representation of some kind sooner or later."

Nora wrinkled her nose at him, not liking

the way that sounded at all. "Kind of like a vulture circling in the sky, knowing that in time, something's going to croak and it'll be good eating."

"That's a disgusting analogy, but I suppose it works on a certain level. I prefer to consider it being in the right place at the right time."

She let a pause rest between them as she privately considered what he'd revealed and wondered if his life was as he'd hoped it would turn out. To her, this kind of existence seemed horribly inadequate and toxic, but as Natalie was fond of pointing out, Nora had a habit of judging everyone else's life by her own yardstick.

"If these people aren't your friends who do you hang out with on your downtime?" He gave her a sardonic look and she was reminded of their first encounter. "Wait, I remember—you don't have downtime. You don't even take time out for a vacation," she finished dryly and grabbed a glass of champagne from the smartly dressed waiter passing by.

He smirked. "You have a good memory."

She returned the smirk. "I do. Ridiculously so, it seems." Nora sipped her champagne, then asked, "So, why do you hate roses so much?"

"Excuse me?"

Nora tapped her temple lightly. "The ridiculously sharp memory strikes again. There's a reason you hate roses. What is it?"

He looked ready to change the subject, but he surprised her with an answer. "My dad. It was his flower of choice. The more exotic the better. Women thought when my dad sent them roses that they meant something to him, but the truth was, they were just one of many."

"Your dad's a player, huh?"

"The worst kind."

How sad. Nora couldn't imagine having such a man for a father. Her dad was a grump, but at least he wasn't chasing every skirt in town.

"Aren't you supposed to mingle or something?" she teased, purposefully lightening the mood.

"That I am. Thanks for reminding me." The corners of his mouth played with a full-fledged smile and she marveled at how handsome he'd become. From a gangly boy to a broad-shouldered man, she mused dangerously, sipping her champagne as Ben eased his way through the crowd to talk with an acquaintance. It didn't matter that he hobbled on crutches; his confidence was alluring.

She tore her gaze away from him, perturbed that he managed to impress her without even trying. Emmett's Mill needed someone like Ben. She jerked imperceptibly at the ludicrous direction of her thoughts and finished her champagne. This was Ben's world, not some forgotten town in the California foothills. And this was not Nora's world. The two didn't blend.

As if the universe needed to prove this point to Nora, a man in a sharp black designer tuxedo entered into her space and his presence immediately set Nora's teeth on edge. His gaze slid over Nora's figure in a way that made her feel as if she should go wash, and for all his outward polish Nora could almost see the corruption coming off him in waves. Buster, the egg deliveryman, had more character in his worn overalls than this man. Nora smiled politely but refrained from joining in the conversation and was relieved when he sauntered off to find someone else's ear to bend.

"Again…not a friend," Ben said when he returned, looking almost as relieved as Nora that the man had left.

"I know," she replied simply. Somehow she'd been certain that Ben would never call someone like that a friend. Gracing him with a warm smile, she slipped her arm through his and he drew her intimately closer as if they truly were a couple instead of what they were, which was infinitely harder to explain. Snugged against him, Nora felt she belonged there. It was a wonderful if startling feeling, and one she wasn't ready to relinquish.

THEY WERE HALFWAY to their table when Ben heard his name. He turned and swallowed a grimace when he realized who was coming at him with a speed that should've been impossible in the blue dress clinging to her body.

Nora must've felt him tense for she glanced at him inquiringly, but he didn't have time to explain that a former lover was heading straight for him, no doubt to gauge his and Nora's relationship. Elise Birkeland was a woman who loved a fair bit of competition and enjoyed considering Ben the prize. Ordinarily he didn't mind the game but tonight he wasn't interested.

"Benjamin," she purred, her native Norwegian accenting his name with a distinctly foreign flavor. She walked straight to him without sparing Nora a glance from her glacial blue eyes, though her gaze swept his injury briefly as if it were not serious enough to warrant much curiosity. "You do not call. It's impolite." She pouted even as she slipped her arms around his neck before he could thwart her intention. "I don't like to be ignored."

"What a coincidence," Nora bristled beside him, drawing both their attention. "Neither do I."

Elise lifted one perfectly arched light brown brow as if amused and allowed Ben to disengage himself from her grasp. "My apologies. I didn't realize you were together," she said with an air that was only mildly apologetic.

"We're not," Nora retorted coolly despite the fire Ben recognized burning behind her eyes. "Together, that is."

Elise angled a look at Ben, who was enjoying Nora's barely contained territorial clutch a little too much and shrugged. "Perhaps when you are not so indisposed?" she asked.

"Perhaps." He inclined his head in a noncommittal gesture, but had a feeling he should've chosen his words more wisely. Elise's beauty didn't hold the same appeal any longer. Her pale hair and light blue eyes looked washed out in comparison to the woman nearly vibrating with life beside him, drawing every set of male eyes in the room to her earthy beauty.

Elise nodded in sardonic deference to

Nora and floated away, another target in her sights, Ben completely forgotten.

"Client, acquaintance or unknown?" Nora asked, a subtle cut to her tone.

"We used to date off and on. Why? Do I sense jealousy?"

She straightened as if realizing how she sounded and scoffed at the very idea. "Get over yourself, Hollister. Where's our table? I'm starved."

He chuckled and led the way toward their seats, annoyed that his crutches prevented him from resting his hand on the small of her back as he would've liked.

Once at the table, he used one hand to pull out Nora's chair and he watched with pleasure as she slid gracefully into it, giving him a subtle smile of thanks for the gentlemanly gesture.

Franklin, Mills & Donovan had bought a table, which always sat eight, and Ben knew all the players occupying the seats. Most were benign to the point of bland, but one in particular was a shark and notorious for ass-kissing, back-stabbing and downright sleazy maneuvers in court but the guy had a winning streak that was close to Ben's and that made him an irritant if nothing else. Seconds later, the object of his irritation appeared out of the throng of people, and Ben replaced the scowl he wanted to show with a tight-lipped courtesy smile in greeting. But the moment Ted Paulsen's eyes alighted on Nora's voluptuous figure and rested a second longer than necessary on the plump swell of her breasts, it took every ounce of self-control not to send him a hard look and growl *back off*. The odd spurt of possession took Ben by surprise and forced him to take a breath and reassess his reaction. Broadening his smile in fake welcome, he extended his hand to his colleague. "Ted, congratulations on the Wilson case. I heard it was a tough one."

"Slam dunk. Shaky prenup," Ted said, shrugging off the congratulations and taking the seat near Nora. His attention swiveled immediately to her rather than to Ben. "I don't believe we've been introduced." He accepted Nora's hand and raised it to his lips, pressing a kiss to the top in a smarmy gesture that caused an incredulous expression to appear on Nora's face.

"Ted Paulsen, Nora Simmons." *Now stop touching her, you idiot, before some of your personality rubs off on her.*

"Nora...beautiful name," he said. "Are you from around here?"

She laughed. "God, no. I can't imagine living in the city. Too many fakes and liars for my taste. How about you?"

Ben wanted to burst out laughing at Ted's stunned look and Nora's accompanying saccharine smile. It took a moment for Ted to realize Nora had seen right through his game and was playing one of her own. Moments later, Ted moved to the opposite side of the table.

"Nicely done," Ben observed lightly.

"Thank you. I hate to say this but I think I've come across every cliché of the wickedly wealthy and those who chase after them all in one night. Is there anyone here who isn't a total waste of oxygen?"

He smothered his laughter, but couldn't stop the smile and managed to gesture discreetly toward another table where an aged woman sat surrounded by those Ben knew to be her protective family. "Over at that table sits one of the richest women in the Bay Area, but aside from this one function, she never goes to these things."

"Why not?"

"Because she hates the people. She calls them 'finks and carpetbaggers.'"

Nora giggled and angled a look. "So why does she come to this one?" she whispered.

"Because she believes in the cause. Staunchly. She's never given a reason for her stalwart support, but something tells me she can empathize with the children who seek shelter within Poppenshier House."

Nora's expression softened. "That's amazing that she shares her wealth with those less fortunate. I wish more people were like her."

He inclined his head but his forehead wrinkled as unwelcome comparisons to his grandfather surfaced. Ada Willows could give millions to help someone, but B.J. had given the only thing he had—his time. Both were noble in their own way but Ben hadn't recognized this fact. Nora had. He glanced surreptitiously her way and his pulse quickened just having her by his side. His feelings posed a significant problem, the analytical side of his brain railed, but he wasn't interested in listening. Right now he wanted to focus on Nora.

The evening passed quickly, but unlike evenings in the past where Ben kept a constant watch on the time, waiting for the first opportunity to politely bow out, an evening spent with Nora felt like time well spent and he wanted more.

"That was actually better than I thought it

was going to be. Honestly, I was afraid it was going to be a ridiculous bore but I had a good time," Nora remarked as they made their way to the car. "It isn't very often I get to wear this dress and you're not a bad date. All in all, I'd say the trip was worth the gas money."

He laughed. "Glad to hear it. What now? Head back?"

"Well, I was thinking we could stop by your apartment and change because as much as I love this outfit, my feet are killing me."

"Absolutely. Did you bring a change of clothes with you?"

"Yep."

He unlocked the car. "Then to the apartment we go."

"Great."

Was that a tremor in her voice? Did she sense the difficulty he was having keeping his thoughts away from what he most wanted? God help him but he wanted to seduce the woman in the worst way and he was fast losing sight of the reasons why it was a bad idea.

## CHAPTER THIRTEEN

NORA FOLLOWED Ben into his apartment and gratefully slipped out of her shoes. She groaned as she wiggled her toes and blood returned to the poor little digits that had been cramped into the fashionable little torture devices pretending to be designer heels. Rarely was Nora a subscriber to the tenet "Sacrifice your body for fashion," but tonight she'd wanted to look every inch the sophisticated woman on Ben's arm. And the fashion gods required the sacrifice of her baby toe on each foot apparently, but a covert glance at Ben revealed her sacrifice had not been in vain.

The man who prided himself on being contained and orderly in all aspects of his life was fumbling with the corkscrew on a bottle of vintage wine. Granted, he was trying to balance on crutches while trying to accomplish his goal, but Nora could almost see the tremble.

She'd most certainly made his eyes cross.

Unfortunately he wasn't the only one. Ben took her breath away each time he pinned her with those intense gazes. They rendered a woman defenseless and that was simply not fair. Sort of like declawing a cat and then throwing the poor feline outside to fend for itself against…a bear.

"Need help?" she offered, wanting to laugh but unable to because of the flutters in her belly.

"Uh, no…well, maybe," he admitted, pursing his lips in agitation as the corkscrew slipped out of his grasp to clatter on the countertop. She took the bottle and returned it to the counter, not sure alcohol was needed; she already felt intoxicated. He watched her cautiously. "What are you doing?"

"I'm not sure," she answered, running the tip of her tongue across her top lip. "But I think I need to get you out of my system and there's only one way I can think of to do that."

His eyes darkened. "Which is?"

"This." She latched her lips onto his and nearly knocked him into the sink, both crutches clattering to the floor as he wound his arms around her, crushing her to him.

Coherent thought—and any counsel as to why this may be a bad idea—fled her mind, and her body took over. Despite his injuries, he managed to hoist her onto the counter and, without stopping the ravenous kiss, her legs went around his waist, drawing him ever closer to that hot heat radiating from her center and spreading to her limbs.

Ben broke the kiss with a savage groan as if the action had cost him. "I don't think this is a good idea," he whispered, but his gaze seared into hers, demanding more.

She dragged his head back down to hers, saying breathlessly, "So don't think."

"Right," he quickly agreed and claimed her mouth again, his tongue slipping inside and ruthlessly teasing her with the promise of what else he wanted to do to her. She moaned and her hands went straight to his pants, making quick work of the clasp and ripping his shirt free of his waistband, so eager she was to touch the flesh only inches away from her questing fingers. His stomach muscles clenched as her palms spread across his belly and hungrily climbed, buttons popping as she divested him of the cumbersome fabric.

"Nora?" he murmured against her mouth, his voice ragged and aroused. "Are you sure? I don't want to do anything that—"

She jerked away from him and gripped his loose lapels. "For the love of God, just shut up and kiss me!"

It was at that moment Ben decided to follow Nora's terse advice and forget about the warnings in his head blaring above the rush of erotic sensations. A wild, hot need burned and ravaged him until all he could see, hear or feel was Nora in his arms.

He didn't notice the pain in his rib or the soreness in his lungs or even the clumsiness of his cast. All he felt was Nora.

They made their way to the bedroom slowly and a bit awkwardly but neither seemed to mind. Soon Nora unzipped her red dress and let it pool at her feet before modeling the delicate black, lacy demi-cup bra-and-panties set that looked straight out of the *Victoria's Secret* catalog. Immediately his heartbeat began thumping wildly against his chest.

"God, you're something," he said as she straddled him gently, keeping most of her weight on his hips and away from his injured side.

"You're easily impressed," she said playfully, pulling her hair free from the pins so that it fell in waves around her shoulders.

"No," he clarified, anchoring his hands on

her waist, loving the way the moonlight dusted her blond hair with silver highlights. "I'm not."

Nora paused, as if letting his simple statement sink in, and then she slowly smiled. "Good to know," she said, her voice low and husky. Then she added devilishly, "Neither am I."

Ben sucked in a sharp breath as she did a sensual grind against the swollen ridge in his loosened pants, and he knew if he made it through tonight he might just touch heaven.

He rolled, wincing when his side protested, and bringing Nora to rest beneath him. He loved the feel of that superior position until his heavy cast made him feel less like Casanova and more like Quasimodo with a concrete block on his foot.

"Ouch," Nora said, wiggling away from the hard plaster rubbing against her leg. She eyed him. "Let's go back to the way we were. With me on top."

He grimaced. "This isn't working out how I planned."

She arched a brow playfully. "Planned, eh? And here I thought we were being spontaneous."

Instead of answering, he dipped down and

claimed her lips softly, nibbling the pouty flesh, determined to make sure he wasn't the only one drowning in sensation and enjoying every minute of it.

They rolled again, returning Nora to the top, and as she unclasped her bra, freeing her breasts, any reservations he may have held disappeared like wisps of smoke in a stiff breeze. God, she was perfect. And for this moment, she belonged to him.

Danger whispered at the heady thought, but he was too far gone to listen. Pausing long enough to reach into his bedside drawer to grab a condom, he ripped the foil with shaking hands and tried not to think of how she affected him but all he could think, smell or see was Nora and he couldn't seem to get enough.

THE NEXT MORNING Nora awoke with a start, momentarily disoriented by her foreign surroundings. A soft snore beside her sent warmth crawling into her cheeks as she slowly turned, clutching the sheet to her naked body to stare at Ben. Heated memories of a torrid night filled her mind and she was caught between wanting more and fleeing the room.

It'd been her idea, but honestly, what had

she been thinking? She rubbed her palm against one eye and sighed softly so as not to wake him, then slid out of bed carefully. She needed a shower and coffee right away to clear the cobwebs in her head that were clouding her judgment. As she padded silently to the bathroom and shut the door, a part of her was wondering why she wasn't snuggled up to the brawny man for a repeat performance.

Because this was a bad idea, her conscience screamed, kicking to life with a vengeance. This was exactly the kind of impetuous maneuver that had got her involved with a married man. She leaped before looking and ended up flat on her face because there'd been no one there to catch her.

She knew Ben wasn't married—wasn't even remotely attached—but tangling with him was worse because she knew from the get-go that he had no desire to stay. Ben fitting in with the small town of Emmett's Mill was as ludicrous and unlikely as Natalie suddenly turning into an exhibitionist and running through the town square naked as a jaybird. But last night had been…phenomenal. And she wasn't just talking about the sex, although that had been sizzling and would most likely ruin her for anyone else in the foreseeable future.

Seeing Ben in his element—confident, secure and knowledgeable—had caused an insidious change in her brain about the man. He no longer seemed arrogant and distant, but someone who was solid in his convictions and didn't care who disapproved. God, he was a man after her own heart. Scary thought, that.

Great. She had to go and ruin the image she was fostering of him. What now? Did they pretend as if nothing had happened? As if they hadn't just rocked each other's world…three times?

She stepped into the steaming shower and let the water sluice over her, content just to let her concerns wash down the drain for the moment.

Irresponsible seemed to be her middle name.

After a quick scrub, she shut off the shower and wrapped herself in a thick white towel. She was prepared to sneak back into the room to retrieve the change of clothes she'd brought last night, but as she opened the door, Ben greeted her with an appreciative grin. "If I didn't have this cast I might've joined you," he said, bending down to nuzzle her neck.

Her eyelids fluttered shut as her heartbeat leaped into her throat but good sense had her sidling out of his reach. "We have to get going. I have a crew coming at noon," she said, throwing a brief smile his way and running from the bedroom.

"Nora, wait," he called, but she'd disappeared into the spare bedroom and shut the door. Leaning against it and clutching her clothes to her chest, she squeezed her eyes shut against the pictures in her head of last night's romp. A knock sounded. "Nora? What's wrong?"

"Nothing."

A pause. "Then why are you hiding behind a door?"

"I'm not hiding. I'm getting dressed. I like a little privacy."

"O-kay," he said, clearly puzzled by her actions, and she didn't blame him. She wasn't making much sense, but that wasn't what was important at the moment. What was important was that they both returned to their senses, and she certainly couldn't do that with him unwittingly enticing her to throw him to the floor and have her wicked way with him. A shudder of delight rocked her body at the thought. *Stop that!* The point of last night was to get him out of her system, but it didn't seem as if she'd achieved her goal. If anything, he was more firmly entrenched in her mind than ever before. *Good going.*

She opened the door to find him still standing there, leaning casually against the doorjamb on his uninjured side. A pang of concern followed as she considered that perhaps sex hadn't been advisable for his recovery. Doc Hessle probably hadn't thought to mention that little bit of advice. "You okay?" She gestured to his side. "Nothing…broken?"

"No more than I started out. How are you?"

"I'm fine," she bluffed, walking past him. "But you better get dressed because we really have to get going."

He pushed off. "I have a better idea," he said, moving much too quickly for a man who was supposed to be incapacitated. He grabbed her by the waist and pulled her to him. Her breath escaped in a little girlie gasp and his eyes dilated at the sound. "Let's go back to bed."

She tried to put on a stern face, but it was hard to hold on to when she was practically nodding her head in agreement. "We shouldn't."

"I agree," he said, surprising her.

"You agree?"

"Absolutely." He started making his way back to the bedroom, pulling her with him.

"This is a terrible idea but as terrible ideas go, I think it's pretty damn fantastic. We're good together, Nora. Sinfully good. And let's just say, it's my turn to get *you* out of my system."

"Oh," she said in a breathless whisper, privately delighted by his husky growl and the way his hard body responded so eagerly to her own. "I have appointments," she countered weakly, licking her lips in anticipation of the carnal promise she read in his eyes. "Lots of them."

"Cancel."

"It's not that simple," she protested even as he pushed her onto the bed, the forcefulness sending her heart racing. He silenced her last objection by pressing his mouth over hers, his tongue slipping and darting inside as his hand closed over her braless breast and squeezed possessively. Her last thought was lost on a moan as his mouth cleared a path to the sensitive skin of her neck, nipping and sucking gently while the stubble on his chin sent goose bumps chasing the waves of desire, clamping down on any sense.

She'd pay for this later but she'd savor it now.

## CHAPTER FOURTEEN

By THE TIME they returned to Emmett's Mill, the day had long since passed, but thanks to a quick phone call to Sammy, the work that had been scheduled was finished and Nora spent the day with Ben. It'd been hedonistic and wonderful, but as the sweat dried and the heated moments cooled, Nora realized she might never get enough of Ben Hollister. That smacked of trouble, she thought ominously, uncomfortable with the one-way road she was traveling. It wasn't as if Ben was staring into her eyes professing his feelings for her. Not that she wanted him to exactly. Rarely did she respect any man who fell at her feet, but she wouldn't be adverse to a little show of affection rather than simple lust.

"I guess I'll take off," she said, gathering last night's clothes from the trunk of Ben's car, not quite sure what to say after the day she'd had. They were no longer strangers, but she still felt as if she didn't know the man, and awkwardness was setting in. "Do you need anything for tomorrow?"

His gaze narrowed seductively and she had to look away, her body reacting in a primal way to that silent signal. "I can think of only one thing I need," he said.

"Well, I wasn't one of the choices," she retorted, shouldering her overnight bag and wincing as the heel of one of her fancy shoes dug into her back. "I meant things like food, toilet paper, essentials."

"I could argue having you naked in my bed is essential but something tells me you're not in the mood."

"Perceptive."

"So I've been told."

Time to set the record straight. "Look, Ben, today was fun but I need to focus. I missed a whole day of work to…" *devour your perfect body like a starving woman.* She drew a deep breath and finished quickly, "You know, and that's not my style. Time to get back to reality."

The subtle flex of his jaw belied the amusement in his expression and she knew she'd just bruised his ego with her rejection. But he surprised her when he said, "Fine."

"Fine?" she repeated, watching him closely. "Your feelings aren't hurt?"

He gave her a patronizing stare. "Nora, it takes more than that to hurt my feelings. I'm a lawyer, remember?"

"Ah, right. So we're good then?"

He chuckled but the sound held a ragged edge. "We're as good as we'll ever be, I suspect. I was going to ask you to stay for dinner, but if you need to go I understand."

The feminine part of her whined and pouted at his offer, knowing she'd cave if only to get that part to shut up so she could think clearly. "You could still ask, I suppose," she said slowly.

His expression brightened momentarily, illuminating those impossibly green eyes until she had to tear her gaze away. She reminded herself that falling for Ben was the worst thing she could do at this juncture in her life, but there was no denying the tingle in her toes at the thought of spending more time alone with him.

"Would you like to stay for dinner?"

She nodded. "I could eat."

"Glad to hear it. I've got all this food and as I've already proved, I can't cook on these crutches. I could use your help."

Oh criminy. He wasn't asking her to stay for dinner because he couldn't bear to spend a night apart—he needed a cooking assistant.

She couldn't help the starch in her spine as she nodded curtly. "I suppose that fits within my job description."

"I believe it does," he agreed, further inciting her indignation until he added with quiet honesty, "But you don't *have* to stay. I was hoping you might *want* to stay…as a friend."

A friend? Her heart melted a little even as he gave her what sounded like a classic line. "Are we friends, Ben?" she asked, peering at him curiously.

He took a moment to answer and when he did, her heart disintegrated into a useless puddle. "I don't know what we are exactly, but I know you're unlike any woman I've ever met and I crave your company. I'm not just talking about your body either, in case you're wondering. Although that's high on my list of desirables. It's just not everything."

The man had talent. "Yes, I'll stay for dinner. Just dinner, though," she reminded him sternly, though her teeth ached just saying it. "I need to get my head straight and I can't do that with you touching me."

One eyebrow lifted sardonically. "You've made yourself clear, Nora. I don't need to be told twice. Just dinner."

An inexplicable sense of disappointment

followed and she wanted to slap herself silly for acting like such a girl. She sure as hell couldn't say one thing and then act disappointed because she got what she wanted.

Where was the harm in a little dessert? A suspiciously female voice whispered as they walked into the house. Dessert was a complication, she told herself, but Nora couldn't help the train of her thoughts with such a nice view of Ben's behind in front of her. She knew firsthand what that flesh felt like beneath her palm and the memory made her insides tremble with need.

Lord. She must have the resolve of a drug addict. She couldn't even rein in her own thoughts on the subject. How pathetic. She inhaled a short breath and told herself all she had to remember was that Ben wasn't here to stay and she wasn't interested in looking when she couldn't buy.

Yeah right, she snorted with the delicacy of a truck driver. Tell that to her raging hormones.

"Just dinner and then I'm outta here," she reminded him. Or was it to convince herself?

NORA, BEN REALIZED, was a terrible cook.

"I never said I was handy in the kitchen," she said defensively as they stared at the rice she'd been put in charge of making. She wrinkled her nose at the gummy, gluelike gunk in the pot and shrugged. "I eat out a lot."

He chuckled as he lifted the pot from the stove and placed it in the sink. "I can see that," he said, filling the pot with water so the rice didn't stick. "How is it you grew up with two older sisters and your mom and you never learned to cook?"

"There was never a need. Natalie or my mom always did the cooking. Plus, a few incidents like this kinda helped push me out of the kitchen. Once I was in charge of making meatballs but I forgot to cook the rice and I cooked the meat too long. Anyway, well, it turned out to be meat loaf with crunchy rice inside. It was gross. No one wanted a repeat of that so I was kicked out of the kitchen." She moved to help Ben remove the casserole from the oven. Once it was safely on the counter to cool, she went to the fridge to take out a bottle of white wine that was chilling. "And once I was out on my own, I ate a lot of Ramen noodles for a while."

Ben gestured to the plates and she retrieved them. "I love cooking. Helps clear my head," he said. She held the plate while he dished out a heaping spoonful of the cheesy stuff he'd whipped up, and even though the rice was clearly inedible, the casserole looked hearty enough.

"In the dining room?" she asked and he nodded.

Nora carried the plates and silverware to the table and then returned with the wine and two glasses.

"Smells good," she admitted, spearing a piece of chicken and twirling the cheese around it as broccoli and other vegetables spilled out from under the thin crust. "But here comes the real test."

The fork disappeared into her mouth and the resulting groan of surprise sent erotic thrills down his body. Chagrined at his own lack of restraint, he focused on his own meal. "Good?" he asked, taking a bite.

"Damn good," she admitted a tad grudgingly. "Where'd you learn to cook like this?"

"College," he answered. "No one in my fraternity could cook, and I was the only one who didn't run home to my parents for a home-cooked meal. I spent a lot of holidays perfecting my methods."

She swallowed and toyed with a pea before taking another bite. The silence told him she was thinking about his last statement. Their lives were so different. Nora had never learned to cook because she was surrounded by family who did it for her; he'd learned to cook because no one else would.

"Tell me what it was like growing up with a silver spoon in your mouth," she said with a sudden smile, and he knew she was trying to keep the conversation light. He was thankful for her effort and decided to share a little. "It's not so different than most childhoods, except I didn't grow up around any blackberry bushes," he teased, referencing their first encounter all those years ago.

She blushed but managed to add, "Yeah, that was painfully obvious."

He chuckled. "You know, you looked like such a wild child that day. Almost like a pixie with your long hair tangled and knotted. I'd never seen anyone like you. Fearless even at ten."

"You probably say that to all the girls," she murmured.

"No, I don't," he said in all honesty. Her spirit demanded nothing less. "Nora, I'm not the type of man to fill a woman's head with pretty lies."

A storm built behind her eyes but she nodded. "I get that. It's honorable in a way. Is that why your last girlfriend didn't stick around?"

He sighed. "In a manner of speaking. I told her I didn't believe in marriage." Or love for that matter, but he kept that revelation behind his teeth. "And she had different goals, ones that included marriage and children. We went our separate ways."

"Why don't you believe in marriage?"

"Because evidence that it doesn't work crosses my desk every day and I get to clean up the mess they leave behind. Assets, financial declarations, custody disputes. The wreckage of a union created by a brief hormonal surge is enough proof for me that marriage is an outdated concept."

His gaze dropped to her fork as she idly played with her food. "Something wrong?"

She looked up and he saw the disappointment in her eyes, although she tried to hide it. "No. Everything's fine."

"Are you sure?"

"Yes. Tell me why you never came back to Emmett's Mill after that one summer."

He drew a short breath. "I tried. My father wouldn't let me."

"Why not?"

"Because my father hated his parents. The only reason he let me visit that one summer was because he and my mother were finalizing the divorce and didn't want me hanging around while they fought over the details. I suppose it was a blessing."

"Did you want to come back?" There was a wealth of emotion behind her question, but Ben wasn't sure where it was coming from.

"Yes."

She seemed to relax subtly as if the answer was exactly what she needed to hear. "Each summer I waited for you to return, but you never did. It was a stupid childhood crush, but I had it bad for you."

"Really?" His heart rate quickened, remembering how many times he replayed that small moment in time when, as children, their lips touched. He caressed her cheek. "How do you feel now?"

The look in her eyes gave her away but she managed a nonchalant shrug. "I feel conflicted."

He could relate. "Why?"

"Because we never should've slept together," she replied softly.

He agreed, but he couldn't get himself to say it aloud for he didn't want to acknowledge how quickly they'd complicated their relationship. All he wanted was to taste her skin, feel her body and know her mind. It was distracting and disconcerting, but the desire was there and he didn't quite know what to do with it.

"You may be right, but we can't take it back." *And I don't want to.* He shifted in his chair, striving for a cool demeanor despite feeling hot inside. "We could pretend it didn't happen and make a vow never to do it again, or we could be adults about it and recognize that we're both attracted to each other and deal with our feelings accordingly."

She leveled her stare. "And how do you suppose we deal with our feelings without making things worse?"

"Allow them to run their course."

She startled. "Excuse me?"

"As I've said before, attraction fades as does the euphoric feeling of being in love after the chemical subsides in your brain. We'll just wait it out and then peacefully go our own ways."

Her expression crystallized with cold fury and he realized she might not see things the same way. It was the same look he'd seen on his last lover's face and he knew the drill. But even though he knew what was coming and figured he was prepared, he wasn't ready for the hurt hiding behind her anger.

"Thank you for making your position perfectly clear," she said, standing. "But I'd rather not participate in your *chemical* romance, if you don't mind. From this moment forward, we're business associates. I think by the time you're able to travel and the house is finished, whatever it is I'm feeling will be completely and sufficiently *dead*."

Ben struggled to go after her, but she was too quick for him. Cursing his broken ankle, he hopped to the door in time to see Nora barrel out of the driveway.

All good feelings of the day evaporated. Better now than later, he told himself, shutting the door and returning to the kitchen to clean up the mess. Better now than when they were more attached than they wanted to admit and a drawn-out breakup ensued.

Yes, this was infinitely better. So why did it feel as if he'd just taken a punch to the sternum from a brute with brass knuckles? The answer seemed simple but Ben refused to acknowledge it. Nora was an itch he couldn't seem to scratch because it was deep under the skin. How'd she manage to get in so quickly?

Again the answer was unnecessary. As an attorney he made his livelihood by stoically analyzing the situation between two people so that he could determine the most agreeable resolution. He'd just apply that skill to his relationship with Nora.

He wouldn't think of her golden skin and the way candlelight brought out the rosy hue along her hip bone, and he certainly wouldn't think of the tiny Chinese symbol tattooed on the curve of her left buttock that he couldn't help but nibble and kiss. He'd forgotten to ask what the character meant. Now the opportunity was gone.

Ben finished cleaning the kitchen and headed for bed. Yes, this was a blessing in disguise. He just had to convince his brain of that simple fact and everything would fall into place.

So, Counselor, closing arguments?

*Just one—what the hell are you thinking? That plan is bound to fail. You've never met someone like her—and probably never will.*

# CHAPTER FIFTEEN

BEN WAS ENGROSSED in case files, looking for some kind of precedents that might help him win the Wallace case, when he heard a short knock at the front door. Rising from his desk, he hobbled to see who it was and saw Buster talking with Nora on the front porch.

Nora saw Ben first and gestured to the basket in Buster's hands. "Now you can give that Denver omelet a second chance," she said.

"Breakfast in bed, perhaps?" he asked, hoping to earn a smile but preparing to duck in case she hurled the garden trowel in her hand at his head. Instead she offered a generic smile that was devoid of warmth before leaving him with Buster, who was watching the exchange with avid interest.

"Good luck catching that one," Buster said with a low whistle.

Ben returned his attention to the older man and accepted the basket of eggs. "What makes you think I'm trying to catch her?" he scoffed lightly.

Buster laughed. "Boy, you've got 'the look' written plain as day all over your face. You've got it bad."

"I assure you, there's no look." Ben fought a grimace, knowing the man meant well, but Buster made it sound as if he'd caught some kind of disease. "We're just client and employer with some slightly friendly overtones," he tried to explain but even to his own ears it sounded lame.

"I call 'em as I see 'em, that's all. Enjoy them eggs. There's more where that came from."

"I appreciate that you're honoring a debt but I think you've satisfied what you owed my grandfather. Let's call it even."

Buster shook his head. "We ain't square till we're square. See you next week."

Ben tried again, but Buster was already in his truck, waving, and then he was gone.

Nora appeared from around the corner and leaned against the side of the house. "You might as well get used to it—he's not going to stop. It's just how people are around here," she said. "How much longer does Buster have on his barter contract?"

Ben groaned. "Another six months."

"That's a lot of omelets."

He skewed an annoyed look her way. "Yeah, tell me about it." What was he going to do when he sold this place? Throw in a free egg-delivery service to sweeten the deal to whomever bought it? "How's the yard coming along?"

She shrugged. "Come and see for yourself."

Ben negotiated the stairs carefully and hobbled after her. He'd been too busy with the Wallace case to spend much time staring out the window today, but it was apparent by the amount of progress she was making, she didn't waste time.

There was still work to do, but the yard was shaping up nicely. The old lawn—if that patch of crabgrass and dried weeds could be called that—had been torn out and a new sprinkler system was going in; the fountain was gone temporarily for refurbishing, and Nora was in the process of trenching for the small koi pond. Adding the fish had been a stretch, but once Nora explained that an exotic feature in the garden always caught people's attention, he agreed to it, though he was still a little uncertain about having fish in his side yard.

"It's a good thing I have a pretty solid

imagination, Simmons," he said, "because this is a mess."

"It's not a mess," she retorted. "It's a work in progress. I just ordered the gazebo. It should be here in a week or two. I can't wait to put it in."

"Gazebo?" he asked, not quite remembering that detail.

She busied herself with gathering her tools. "Yeah, remember? The gazebo that overlooks the herb garden."

He stared harder, searching his memory. "I think I missed something. Did you say herb garden?"

She made a sound of impatience. "Yes, herb garden. It's all in the plans I showed you. You should pay better attention. If you had a problem with it, you should've said something before now. The supplies are already ordered."

"Why would I want a herb garden?" he asked, refusing to let the topic go. "I don't know the first thing about growing herbs, nor would I want to, and while you made a solid point with the koi pond, I don't think a herb garden is going to help sell the house."

Nora stuffed her tools in the back of her truck and glowered, muttering something highly uncomplimentary as she stalked by him. "I disagree. A herb garden that isn't tended regularly still gives the air a sweet, fresh smell even if you never use the herbs for any real purpose."

"That's ridiculous. Why would I pay for something that has no real purpose?"

"I didn't say it had *no* purpose, I said if it wasn't *tended* for any real purpose. Can't you see the difference?"

He shook his head, perplexed at her logic—or lack thereof. "No."

"Too bad for you, I guess," she said, moving past him until he grabbed her arm. She glared icily. "Remember the last time you grabbed me? It didn't end well for you."

Ben grimaced and released her. "Sorry, I didn't mean to, I just want you to slow down and talk to me. You have me at a disadvantage here." He pointed at his foot. "It's not like I can exactly keep up."

Her expression told him she didn't really care. Displeasure at how their relationship had become antagonistic again made him soften his words.

"Let's start over," he offered, but she only stared warily. "Last night ended badly. I probably could've handled our conversation with a little more tact but I didn't want to lie to you or give you false hope that I was the kind of man who wanted marriage and kids. It's just not me. But I really enjoy your company and I'd like to spend more time with you while I'm here."

"That's your idea of starting over?" she asked incredulously, her tone washing over him in strident waves. When he nodded in earnest, she slapped her thigh. "Well, that explains a lot. You. Are. An. Idiot."

He sputtered. "I am not."

"Only an idiot without a lick of sense in his head would think of telling a woman he's already slept with that he wouldn't mind hanging out and enjoying a little sex on the side while he's stuck in her Podunk town. It's no wonder you can't keep a girlfriend. You've got the social skills of a yak. To answer your proposition—so there's no room for misinterpretation—the thought of having sex with you now is as desirable as having a nail pounded into my foot. Your arrogance is only outmatched by your colossal ego and I can't imagine anyone wanting to spend more than ten minutes in your exalted company unless you were paying them—and even then, the sum would have to be pretty exorbitant. Are we clear, Benjamin Hollister?"

*Perfectly.* He pulled her into his chest with

his free hand and claimed her sassy mouth. She gasped—and perhaps even growled, he wasn't sure, but the sound sent a zap straight to his groin—and met the thrust of his tongue with an aggressive parry as they tangled with a violence that made his knees weak. Just when he thought he was going to have to drag her to the ground, she tore her mouth away from his and gave him a savage push. His back hit the side of the house, but he was otherwise unharmed.

"Don't do that again," she said, her breath coming in short pants until she could draw a deeper lungful of air. They stood staring at each other, but Ben refused to acquiesce to her demand. He wanted to kiss her and more. It was reckless and stupid to push the issue; she'd stated her preference—though her reaction to his kiss completely belied that statement—and he should, by all rights, back off. But he wouldn't. Something about her tied him in knots with wanting and it wasn't just her body. By God, he wished it were. It would simplify things by half.

"You can pretend you don't feel anything, Nora, but I won't buy it," he said, his heart rate finally slowing to a normal pace. "Whether you like it or not, there's something between us and I'm not afraid to see where it goes."

She swallowed as if afraid of the words she was trying to say. Finally she straightened and said with deliberate calm, "Ben, I know exactly where it will go...and where it will end. I'm choosing to end it now. I expect you to abide by my decision or I quit."

NORA SAT on the porch swing at her father's house and listened as her sisters' voices floated through the open window as Natalie and Tasha argued with their father about a subject that—by the sound of it—held neither their father's nor Nora's interest. She'd become accustomed to her sisters' squabbling since Tasha had come home a year or so ago and had usurped Natalie as the head of the siblings. Under normal circumstances Nora would have gleefully thrown in her two cents, but today, picking a side on any argument other than the one she was currently fighting didn't hold a candle.

Tucking her leg under her, she let her gaze drift over the tree line to the setting sun, comforted by the familiarity of her childhood home. A forlorn sigh escaped just in time for her sister Tasha to hear it.

"I didn't know you were here," she admonished gently. "You should've come in. I could've used your help in there."

"What's going on?" Nora asked, more out of courtesy than real interest. Her brain was elsewhere. "I heard you guys arguing."

Tasha exhaled loudly and shook her head. "Natalie thinks Dad should stop drinking, and I don't think it's a big deal. She found your beer and threw a fit."

Nora rolled her eyes, annoyance flaring bright. "She needs to stop focusing on Dad and worry more about her own life. He's fine. She needs to stop mothering him. If Mom's staring down at us right now, she's probably shaking her head and wondering how she managed to raise such a nitwit."

A small giggle from Tasha followed before she sobered, saying in Nat's defense, "She's just trying to do what's right. No doubt she felt she had to pick up the slack while I was gone. Do you think Dad should stop drinking?"

Nora leveled a look at her sister. "Only if he wants to. He's not an alcoholic. Natalie needs to relax."

Tasha nodded. "Glad to hear we're on the same page. I might need reinforcements later. Now that that's out of the way, what's up, little sis? It's not like you to hang out by yourself." Nora answered with a small shrug, but Tasha saw right through her. "Give me some credit. I can tell something's eating at you," she said.

"Nothing I can't handle," Nora said with more confidence than she felt. "Just a little work situation. I have a client who's a little too full of himself."

"Is this the same guy you were talking about a couple of weeks ago?"

"The same."

"Is he coming on to you or something?"

Nora's cheeks heated and she mumbled, "Or something."

"Ah," Tasha murmured in understanding. "You like him, don't you?"

Nora stared morosely and thought to lie, but she needed to talk with someone and her older sister was a good start. "Yeah, you could say that, I suppose. I think I've had a crush on him since I was ten, only it took until now to realize it."

"So what's the problem?"

"Everything. He's a jerk. Of course, he didn't seem like a jerk until recently and I realized he'd always been a jerk. He just hid it well enough for me to think he was decent."

"Sounds manipulative," Tasha observed. "Did you come to this realization before or after you slept with him?"

Nora whipped her gaze to her sister's, shocked she'd been able to zero in on that particular point. "After," Nora finally answered. "And I'm really mad and achingly disappointed he's not who I wanted him to be."

"Who did you want him to be?"

*A keeper.* Nora swallowed the response that instantly flew to mind and shrugged. "It doesn't matter. Whatever I wanted...he wasn't."

THE SOUND OF A TRUCK rumbling into the driveway immediately had Ben shuffling to the window in the hopes that it was Nora but he was disappointed to see it was not.

Pushing open the screen door, he signaled to the man Ben recognized as Nora's backhoe buddy as he headed for the yard.

"Nora can't make it today," he explained. "Said something about not wanting to see your face. Boy, you've done put your foot in it, haven't ya?" He chuckled and Ben colored. "But don't stress, she told me what she wants done, so no worries about the job."

He wasn't worried about the job. "She's not coming at all?" he asked gruffly.

"Nope."

Great, he thought sourly. "Did she say anything else?"

The man did a show of searching his memory, then replied with great relish, "Nope."

Ben's gaze narrowed. "You don't like me much, do you?"

"No, I don't, and I'll tell you why. I've never seen Nora all tied up in knots over a guy. Whatever you did, it was enough to change the woman I've known my entire life and it wasn't for the better. So the sooner you're out of all our hair, the better, I say. Things can get back to normal around here."

"Let me guess, old boyfriend?" Ben assumed, trying not to think of Nora in an intimate tangle with the man.

"Wrong. Best friend. Name's Sammy Halvorsen. And I know you're the fancy lawyer who's here to offload his family's house for a quick buck. Nora has a soft heart for all her bluster. Take a word of advice and leave as soon as you can. We don't need people like you in Emmett's Mill and neither does Nora."

"Nora's an adult, she can make up her own mind," he answered calmly, though a slow, angry burn was searing his chest. "I'd thank you for the advice if it were needed, but it's not, so in the interest of preserving our working relationship, I'll just ask you to mind your own business and leave it at that. What happens between Nora and me is private and will remain private. Do we understand each other?"

Sammy's sardonic chuckle made Ben want to jab him in the gut with his crutch. "You've got a lot to learn about small towns," he said. "Nothing's private. If you're planning to stay you'd better get used to it."

He scoffed. "What makes you think I'm staying?"

"Because you seem to have a thing for Nora and nothing short of dynamite is going to blast her out of this town. She has something you'll never understand—pride in her roots. That's why you're going to leave and she's going to let you."

Ben swallowed at the man's uncanny insight, but refused to give him the satisfaction of knowing he'd hit a nerve. "Well then, I won't keep you from your work," he said coldly, allowing the door to slam behind him.

He didn't want to stay; she didn't want to go. He didn't want the white picket fence and she didn't want a relationship that didn't hold the promise of marriage. She was smart to cut things off; a part of him appreciated her fortitude for ending something that held no future, but every time he considered walking away from her—as he should—he found himself fighting for air. He was scaring himself.

Heading to the office that was beginning to feel more comfortable than his corner office at the firm, he grabbed the phone and prepared to haggle with his client, knowing the battle was a suicide mission; Ed Wallace wasn't only a dumb son of a bitch, he was greedy, too.

He thought of Buster and how the man had integrity in spades yet little cash and wondered how his perception of people may have been altered if, instead of being kept from knowing his grandparents, he had been allowed to see them every summer. Would his view have differed? For the first time in his life, he allowed his mind to briefly consider what it would be like to have a wife. Nora starred front and center in his fantasy and he had to admit it didn't instill the knee-jerk reaction of distaste that usually followed, but he couldn't bear the thought of watching the love shining in her eyes slowly wither and disappear until they were sitting opposite one another in a court-room, haggling over who got the furniture.

And kids? He closed his eyes against the vision that popped into his head of a tow-headed little girl with Nora's spirit and inqui-sitive nature and a boy with his smile.

What was wrong with him? He jumped out of the chair as quickly as his injury would allow and limped out of the room as if that action alone would erase the image stuck in his head. Nothing short of a lobotomy was going to get rid of that tempting vision. And even then…who knows?

# CHAPTER SIXTEEN

THE NEXT DAY, Nora dragged herself out of bed and prepared to go to work, and although she knew she had to face Ben sooner or later, she'd been hoping for later so that when she did see him she didn't do something rash.

And when it came to her mercurial moods, the definition of *something rash* had a wide range of possibilities.

It was time to take Ben to Doc Hessle's for a checkup and since she was Ben's number-one taxi service, it was up to her to get him there.

Of all the stupid scrapes she'd put herself into, this one certainly took the cake. For the first time ever, she was tempted to walk away from the job and refund Ben his money, but her pride prevented her from doing it, so as she climbed into Bettina, she tried not to notice that she'd put a little extra effort in her appearance today, arguing she wanted to look nice for Doc Hessle.

Yeah. That's why she'd dragged out her antique curling iron and tried coaxing her wild hair into some kind of style. Yep. For the doc.

Fine. She did it but for Ben, but only so that he knew right away what he was missing.

Slightly mollified by her logic, she backed out of her driveway and then pulled onto the highway.

As she pulled into Ben's driveway, she saw the work Sammy had finished yesterday and an ill-contained sound of joy escaped her mouth, as the rest of the old shrubbery had been cleared away, and the earth was clean and bare, ready for the plants she had waiting to go into the ground.

Corrinda and B.J. would've been thrilled. A small tear fell from the corner of her eye at the memory of the old coots and it took her a moment to get under control. She didn't want Ben to see her blubbering. The selfish prick would probably think she was crying over him.

And she so wasn't.

Bettina screeched in protest as Nora opened the driver's-side door and popped out of the truck. After promising the old girl a squirt of WD-40 when they got to town, she strode to the front door. She walked inside and hollered.

"Taxi's here, city boy. Get your butt in gear, this ride's taking off in two minutes."

Ben appeared, looking adorably rumpled and disheveled, and she wondered for a split second whether he'd slept in his clothes. But even as she thought it, she stomped the concern down with the vicious intent of a child stepping on a colony of ants collecting food for the winter. He wasn't worthy of her anxiety.

"I overslept," he said, his voice as bleary as his eyes. "I need to shower."

Nora looked at her watch. "Five minutes, no more."

He eyed his cast and shook his head. "I need more time than that to shower with this thing on my foot. It'll take at least five minutes to wrap it up. Unless—" his expression turned suggestive as he added "—you want to help."

She hit him with a scathing look and sniffed. "Take as long as you need. You're the one who has to deal with the doc, not me."

"Forget it. I'll just wash my face real quick."

"And hopefully brush your teeth," she said under her breath, but Ben's look told her he heard her comment just fine. She suppressed a smile and turned her attention to the window facing the side yard, sighing with annoyance at the delay.

"Make yourself at home," Ben said caustically as he slowly disappeared to change.

Resisting the urge to respond by sticking out her tongue, she turned on her heel abruptly and headed for the kitchen to check his food stores. Peeking her head into the fridge, she noted with satisfaction that he was getting low on milk and butter—though not eggs, thanks to Buster's faithful deliveries—and wondered when she'd become so mean. The man had to eat and he was stranded, for crying out loud. If her mom were alive Nora would probably go deaf from the lectures she'd give on being a good Christian.

Well, she'd never been particularly pious, and her mom knew that, but she had to give the woman kudos for never giving up.

A surprise smile lifted her mouth as she closed the fridge. Her mom would've loved Ben. She'd always held out hope her youngest daughter would meet and settle down with a nice boy. Ben gave off that impression—too bad it wasn't real.

Ben reappeared through the breezeway and

she sucked in a hungry gasp at his appearance. On second thought, she mused, deliberately averting her gaze, she preferred the rumpled look over the quickly cleaned one. He smelled like soap and his black hair was shiny from the hasty dousing, which only made him look all the more like some Calvin Klein model. As if he needed help in that department.

The man should seriously rethink his decision to procreate. His babies would be lovely.

"Let's go," she demanded, stalking from the room, determined to get this day over with. "Some of us don't have all day."

"I'm right behind you," he murmured and his tone made her distinctly aware of his hot gaze on her backside.

She whirled and hissed, "And don't stare at my ass!"

He chuckled and smiled, knowing he'd been caught, and the temptation to push him down another hill was only tempered by the secretly giddy pleasure that she affected him the same way he affected her.

At least that part of their relationship wasn't one-sided.

The ride was silent, though Nora was nurturing a wildly destructive hope that Ben might try to strike up a conversation just so she could shut him down. By the time they arrived at Doc Hessle's office, she was sullen and disappointed.

"I'll stay out here," she said in the waiting room, flopping into the nearest chair and refusing to look at Ben as he hobbled to the front desk to talk with the receptionist.

Mabel, the doc's wife, chatted with Ben as if she wasn't aware that he'd completely cut his grandparents out of his life, when Nora happened to know Mabel and Corrinda had been bingo buddies.

Ben disappeared with a nurse and Nora grabbed an outdated *National Geographic* and tried burying her nose in it, but Mabel had spied her and appeared to be in the mood to chat.

Not that the older woman was ever not in a mood to chew the fat—Mabel was the resident gossip—but she seemed overly pleased to see Nora had brought Ben.

"He's a looker, isn't he?" Mabel gushed, prompting Nora to lift the magazine higher to dissuade any further conversation. "Nora Marie, I know you see me. Come over here and chat a minute," she instructed sternly, and Nora grudgingly put the magazine down.

"Isn't there some rule about chatting while working?" Nora asked.

"Not that I'm aware, at least not in this office," she answered with a cheeky grin.

"Maybe there should be," Nora grumbled. "How are you, Mabel? Win anything good lately?"

"Actually, funny that you should ask…I won a really wonderful toaster oven but I already have one I like so I gave it to Sunny Watkins. Since her husband died last year, she said she can hardly bring herself to cook, so I told her a toaster oven was perfect for fixing meals for one."

"That was nice of you," she said.

"We haven't seen you around the senior center much lately. What's got you so busy that you can't play a round of bingo now and then?"

She must've let her gaze stray to where Ben had disappeared, for Mabel immediately got a knowing look. "Oh honey, I don't blame you—he's cuter than a frog's ear. I think he looks a little like B.J., don't you think?"

"Uh, maybe a little?" Nora wondered if Mabel had been a little sweet on old B.J. Harmless flirtation was Mabel's middle name no matter her quarry's age. "Although he doesn't have his integrity," she said under her breath.

Mabel didn't seem to catch Nora's comment and continued to prattle. "I don't know about you, but if I were your age—and single, of course—I'd hook that boy faster than you could blink. He's a major prize. Good-looking, smart and with a fine job, you could do a lot worse." Mabel's voice dropped an octave in the interest of privacy. "And he's single. Not like that last man you set your sights on."

Nora colored and wanted to drop through the floor. No such thing as a secret in a small town. "Yes, well, he has the manners of a dog that hasn't been housebroken. I pity the woman who does try to catch him. She's in for a world of heartbreak."

Mabel looked taken aback. "That's a shame. He's so cute."

"Yeah, so are puppies until they pee on the rug."

Mabel tittered and Nora resisted the urge to roll her eyes. There was more to life than a guy who wasn't hard on the eyes. As Mabel so eloquently pointed out, Nora should know.

Ben walked out with Doc Hessle, and Nora did her best to appear disinterested, bored even, by his return. She checked her watch. "Done? You're still on crutches?" she noted in disappointment.

"Doc says I'm not quite ready for a walking cast yet, but my ribs are healing up nicely."

"Ankles are tricky buggers. Are you staying off it like I told you?"

"More or less," Ben answered, and Nora wanted to snort but didn't because if she did, she'd have to admit she was to blame for some of that activity.

"Well, keep doing what you're doing," Doc advised, and Nora almost choked on her own spit when Ben cast an eager look her way.

"I'm doing my best," Ben answered solemnly like a good boy, and Nora glared. *Oh, puhleeze*. If only Doc Hessle had an inkling as to what Ben hoped to continue doing—mainly her!—he'd probably snap Ben in the ear for getting fresh.

"I suspect another two weeks and you'll be ready for a walking cast. You have great healing capacity," Doc Hessle said, clapping Ben on the back and causing him to hold his smile with difficulty. "Some people take forever to heal from the smallest of wounds, but others mend quickly—that's a sign of a healthy body and good genes."

"Is that your scientific or medical opinion, Doc?" Nora asked wryly.

"Both, smart aleck," the doc retorted, eliciting a wider grin from Ben. He turned to Nora, serious. "You're doing a good thing helping this man out. Think you can hang in there for a little while longer?"

*No*. "As long as he continues to pay me," she answered sweetly.

The doc laughed. "In that case, keep your checkbook handy, Ben. This girl is all business."

Ben arched his brow so that only Nora would catch the subtle meaning, and if it weren't for the doctor standing there, she might've broken his other ankle.

"So are we done here?" she asked, eager to leave. Doc Hessle nodded and she smiled. "Great. Let's get moving. I have work to do."

"You and me both," Ben declared, earning a black look from Nora.

From behind the counter, Mabel made a clucking noise and they turned to find the older woman giving her husband a conspiratorial look. Nora's stomach was uneasy. Those two were up to something. "Mabel, Doc, whatever you two are thinking, you can just forget it because I'm not interested."

"Aw now, Nora, don't be like that," Mabel

said. "I just had a fabulous idea and it wouldn't hurt to hear me out. Jim and I have been looking for a replacement couple for the bingo tournament because we can't make it tonight on account of unexpected plans to have dinner with the Johnsons, but if we give up our spot, we'll be out of the tournament."

"Mabel," Nora said plaintively, shuddering at the thought of spending an entire night at the senior center playing bingo with Ben. "That's kind of last minute. I'm sure Ben already has plans…"

Ben made a fair show of checking his memory and if she hadn't been royally annoyed with him she would've appreciated his playing along but then he ruined any good feelings she had by grinning widely and proclaiming he was free for the night.

"Excellent," Mabel exclaimed, turning to her husband. "We're still in!" She looked at Nora and gave her a bright, thankful smile and that, at least, was genuine. "We really appreciate this. We're in the top tier. I have my sights set on that plasma television. Tonight could be the big night."

Ben arched a brow. "A plasma television at bingo?"

Mabel nodded her head vigorously. "Oh yes, it was donated, of course, but it's a top-of-the-line model that we'd never feel right spending the money on for ourselves but would love to win. Jim likes to watch his *CSI* on a nice screen," she added with a wink. "I'll call Mary Alice—she's the bingo coordinator this round—and let her know that you'll take our place."

Nora's mouth worked but no words actually came out. The woman was a master. Somehow Nora had been roped into playing bingo and she wasn't even sure how it had happened. Doc caught her dumbfounded expression and rubbed her shoulder in understanding.

"You didn't stand a chance, sweetheart. She's been looking for our replacements for weeks. You were in the right place at the right time."

"That's debatable," she grumbled, shooting Ben a look that promised retribution for not helping her out. She sighed. "What time are we supposed to be there?"

Mabel grinned. "Seven sharp, dear. And remember to dress lightly, the air conditioner is having fits again and can't seem to handle all the excitement of bingo night."

Ben's amused smile made her want to plant her foot in his behind. He thought he'd won that round. Well, he'd discover soon enough it was a dubious win, for she doubted a night with the elderly of Emmett's Mill was high excitement for the silver-spooned city boy. By the end of the evening, she'd be the one laughing.

IT TOOK SOME EFFORT but Ben convinced Nora to meet him at the house so they could drive together. Even though he couldn't get himself there it felt good to climb into his car and look across the way and see Nora sitting beside him.

He wasn't sure if it was a deliberate attempt at making him drool or if she dressed like this every time she went to play bingo, but he could barely keep his eyes where they belonged.

She wore a light, gauzy top that exposed the tanned, sultry skin of her neck that he vividly remembered kissing and nipping. Her delighted moans echoed in his memory and his jeans tightened as his groin remembered as well. He shifted discreetly, glad her attention was focused on driving the high-performance sports car and not on the suspicious bulge in his trousers. Light khaki capris and flirty sandals finished the look that was relaxed yet feminine, and her hair was loose and framed her face in beautiful waves. She wasn't wearing earrings but there was a light gloss slicking her lips that made him want to sample that delectable honey one more time. Who was he kidding? One more time? Try a thousand and even then he wasn't sure that would be enough to sate the hunger raging inside him.

They entered the senior center recreation hall and Ben was amazed at how bustling the room was, given the average age of the people inside. There was a blue-haired woman operating a smoothies bar and another couple selling kettle corn, the warm, sweet smell wafting through the air and giving the place a festive feel.

"Lively group, aren't they?" he observed, watching in amusement as a couple two-stepped past them to the music playing in the background. "And nimble," he added as the elderly man dipped his partner as if they were Fred Astaire and Ginger Rogers.

Nora allowed a small smile, but it was clear by the warm reception she wasn't a stranger to this group. "I like bingo," she admitted, moving away quickly before he could comment. He watched as she maneuvered her way to the lead announcer—who must've been Mary Alice—and after a short conversation and a lot of head bobbing, Nora returned with a set of playing boards. She handed him his and gestured to a free spot. "We'd better get a seat. This place fills up fast."

"Who knew bingo was such a draw?" he joked, pausing to pull out her seat before sitting in his own. She hesitated at his gesture but took her seat and scooted closer to the table. "So how do you play?"

"You don't know how to play bingo?" she asked incredulously, but he tried not to take offense. He was fairly certain there were things he could do that she could not.

"Do you know how to play water polo?" he retorted.

"Why would I know how to play water polo?"

"I could ask the same about bingo."

She snorted. "Apples and oranges." Then for reasons he wasn't sure, she switched gears. "All right, let's get down to basics. Mary Alice will select the numbers from the tumbler and read them out loud. You check your playing board for the number and if you've got it, place your chip on the number. Bigger places use a special marker on the playing board but we're not that sophisticated. The middle spot is your free square and then it's up to you to pay attention. When you get five in a row, yell *bingo*."

"Sounds fun," he said with a grin. "Any other special bingo lingo I should know?"

She cracked a smile and shook her head. "Just pay attention. And if you yell bingo, don't knock your chips off the board, because someone will come and check to make sure you're right."

He leaned over to whisper, "I'll bet that's a common problem with this bunch."

She giggled but immediately sobered as if realizing she was having fun and said, "There are people in this room who run 10ks and bike cross-country. Don't let their age fool you. These people don't let a number drag them down."

"Point taken."

"Good. I should also point out that Hugh—" she pointed discreetly to a spry-looking gentleman with waves of white crowning his head "—is a master at jujitsu."

He eyed the man. "Also good to know. Thanks."

Suddenly excitement flared in Nora's eyes and she gestured toward Mary Alice as she took the small stage where the tumbler was sitting on a table. "Get ready to experience senior center bingo, Emmett's Mill style," she added with a superior smile. "I guarantee you've never seen anything like this."

He was ready—or so he thought.

Hours later, he was wiping away the sweat beading on his brow and chanced a glance at Nora who was eyeing her board, memorizing her open spots so that, if by chance her number was called and she got bingo, she could scream it out faster than anyone else in the room. Judging by the past rounds, that was quite a feat. He was sitting in a good spot—he could get a bingo with two different numbers, but so was Nora. Her tongue snaked along her bottom lip and her fingers clenched the tiny chip in her hand and every muscle looked tensed and ready to go at the slightest provocation. If she won, he worried she might shoot out of her chair like a rocket.

It was the final round and the television was on display. Ben wanted to win so he could give it to the doc and his wife, but the competition was fierce.

"Here's the next number," Mary Alice said, pulling a ball from the tumbler. "Everyone ready? Lucky number B-thirteen!"

A bingo sounded from Ben's left amid the loud groans of disappointment and Nora was craning her neck to see who had won. Mary Alice hurried over to double-check the numbers and announced, "No win! Sorry,

Stan. You must've thought I'd said B-seven when I actually called *B-eleven*."

Stan lifted his hands in chagrin, but otherwise seemed to take his mistake well.

"There's still a shot," Nora said, concentrating so hard Ben actually wondered if she was trying to telepathically communicate the numbers she needed to the caller.

"Using the Force?" he asked playfully and he gestured toward her intense expression and clenched fists.

Nora loosened up—a little—and returned to her board. "C'mon D-fourteen or F-twenty. Mama needs a new plasma television."

Ben laughed but Nora's ardent plea to the bingo gods sent a dark thrill twisting through his insides. Mama…she'd make a fun mom. Possibly not the type to be the PTA president, but definitely one all the kids loved because she went out of her way to ensure everyone was having a good time. He pictured her laughing, cuddled with a blond-haired boy and a little girl dancing with a puppy—a snapshot of familial bliss.

Nora gripped his arm and he realized she was pointing wildly at his card. Breaking from his disturbing thoughts, he glanced at his card and realized Nora was saying he'd won.

Holy crap… "Bingo!"

Mary Alice hurried over and after a quick check, declared him the winner of the plasma television.

"I can't believe you won," Nora said, bordering on a dark glower that was completely adorable. He loved her competitive nature—even at a bingo game. "You must have the luck of the Irish," she pouted. "Well, let's go see how to collect your prize."

Ben and Nora went to Mary Alice, and after signing a release stating it was now his property and not subject to return because it was a donated item, Ben asked if he could leave the television overnight because his car wasn't large enough to transport it.

Mary Alice grinned knowingly. "You must be the one with the fancy sports car. I figured as much," she said. "No problem. Here's my number, just let me know when you want to pick it up."

He smiled his thanks and steered Nora to the smoothies bar. "Thirsty?"

"Parched."

"Strawberry banana or strawberry banana?" He read the choices and she laughed. He nodded, saying to the lady behind the counter, "Two strawberry bananas, please."

"Coming right up, handsome."

He caught Nora tossing her hair and fought the urge to plant a kiss straight on her mouth. "C'mon, admit it, you had fun," he teased.

She sent him a cool look. "Of course I had fun. I'm a regular here."

"I gathered from all the warm hellos. Now don't get me wrong because this was an unexpected treat, but you're about three decades too young for this crowd. Why don't you hang out with people your own age?"

He wouldn't have been surprised if she told him to mind his own business but she didn't. She accepted her smoothie and after a sip, answered blithely, "Because unlike people my own age, what you see here is what you get. These folks have lived full lives and no longer see the value of lying. I trust them."

As they walked to the car, he realized her honesty covered a bigger truth—a wound she was protecting. He waited until they were on the highway to return carefully to their previous discussion. "That guy you were seeing—the married one, he hurt you pretty bad, didn't he?" Her guarded expression was all the reply he needed. "What did you like about him? What was so special about him that you let your guard down?"

She sighed and shook her head with a self-deprecating smile. "I don't know. Bad timing. He was funny and confident and sexy. We got along so well, and he never showed any outward signs that he was married. He didn't wear a ring and he never had any pictures in his apartment that I could see that would make me suspicious. And I never asked."

"He had his own apartment?" he asked.

She nodded. "Cute little place in Elk Grove. Later, I learned he kept his own place but he kept the house with his wife in Woodland Hills. Never figured our paths would ever cross."

Ben shook his head at the embarrassment he heard in Nora's voice, hating the guy for hurting her. "You know all guys aren't like him," he reminded her gently, though to what purpose he wasn't sure. She'd already stated her adamant desire to stay away from him.

She forced a chuckle. "A lawyer *and* a shrink? Your clients are so lucky. Listen, Ben, I know all guys aren't like Griffin, but I haven't found another I'm interested in taking a chance on." She chose not to look at him when she said that, and Ben sensed she was lying. She'd been willing to take a chance on him but he'd dropped her as badly as Griffin, with one exception, he defended himself—he'd never promised her a future. Still, he had let her down.

She pulled his car into the driveway of his place, and he invited Nora in for a nightcap. To his surprise, she accepted, though he wasn't about to question her motives. Frankly he didn't care.

Nora wandered into the darkened sitting room and, after lighting a single lamp, relaxed into an overstuffed lounge chair with a sigh. She didn't look like a guest but rather the woman of the household. Ben backed out of the room to clear his head and returned with two glasses of red wine.

She accepted the glass and smiled shyly. "Thanks for going to bingo with me. Mabel and Jim are going to be over the moon that you won that television."

He grinned and savored a swallow of wine. "I'm actually excited about seeing their expressions when I tell them tomorrow. You should come with me."

"Maybe. I have a lot of work to do."

She dipped her head and inhaled the woodsy scent of the wine, enjoying the way the smooth alcohol soothed her tensed muscles and eased her concerns that coming inside was a bad idea. She finished her glass and watched as Ben made his way toward her, unbuttoning the first two buttons of his shirt to expose a glimpse of his smooth chest.

"How's your foot?" she asked, but her gaze was nowhere near his ankle. She knew what lay beneath that shirt and the knowledge teased her senses and messed with her ability to think clearly.

He eased into a wing chair. "Not bad. It feels weak and there's a twinge now and then, but other than that, I guess it's doing better."

She smiled but her mind was far from the doc. She bit her bottom lip. "Glad to hear it." As if suddenly seeing herself and her actions if she stayed, she mustered the strength to end the evening and slowly stood. "I should go," she announced almost painfully.

He nodded as if it was a good idea, but then must've changed his mind, for as she walked past him, he gently grasped her hand and pulled her to him until she was in his lap. It felt entirely too good to be cradled in his arms.

"Ben…"

"Shhh…" he murmured, stealing her breath with the soft press of his lips against hers. "I've been wanting to do this all night," he admitted. "You're so amazing. So unlike any woman I've ever known…" He deepened the kiss with almost savage intensity. She responded greedily, a part of her brain wailing at the lack of control she was exerting, and a second later she turned and straddled his hips, placing her knees on either side of his thighs. He looked into her eyes and she nearly melted at the wonder she saw there. "Woman…" he said, cradling her with both hands. "You're under my skin and I don't know what to do about it."

"That makes two of us," she admitted, sliding her hands up his chest and fighting the purr she felt rumbling in her throat. Too many clothes between them, a voice whispered, and she was inclined to agree. Sliding carefully off his lap, he watched warily as if he was afraid she was going to leave. She smiled and held out her hand. "Let's go complicate things."

He didn't hesitate and accepted her hand. She pulled him out of the chair and smack into her mouth. *A perfect place to be,* she thought fuzzily as desire blotted out anything that didn't involve their bodies rubbing against each other.

They managed an odd kiss-and-stumble to his bedroom before they fell onto the four-poster bed and the gauzy netting draped the bed, but Nora only felt Ben's fingers divesting her of her clothes until she was bare to his hungry gaze, loving the way he seemed to drink her appearance like a starving man. Never had she felt so desired, so wanton yet so safe. With only a few choice curse words as his cast hindered progress, Ben had shucked his own clothing and carefully climbed the length of her body until he was above her, staring down at her as if she were a prize he'd won in battle and meant to treasure. She realized hazily, she could happily drown in a look like that.

"You're so beautiful," he murmured, sealing her mouth with another searing kiss before gently capturing both of her hands and pulling them over her head so that she was helpless to escape even if she'd had the wherewithal to try. The simple action sent a dark thrill spiraling down to her toes and her breath hitched in her throat.

With one hand free, he gently massaged her breast until her nipples puckered painfully, aching for the hot slickness of his mouth. She didn't have to wait long. Seconds later, he descended on her breast, laving it with his tongue until she writhed against the hold he had on her, and her hips bucked against the erection she felt against her thigh. She bit her lip against the urge to beg.

He released her arms and she wound them

around his neck so they could roll together until she was on top.

She grinned devilishly, knowing exactly how to move to put him over the edge, but he surprised her by flipping them again. "Not so fast," he said, exciting her with his control. "You're not getting there yet."

He slid down her body, stopping at the juncture of her thighs, and hooking his arms around her legs, he lifted her until her most private part was exposed and ready for his mouth.

Nora groaned and sank into the pillows as his tongue touched her with alternating strokes that within moments had her panting and gripping the bedcovers against the building crescendo waiting to explode within her body.

She tensed and her heart seemed to stop as stars burst behind her eyes with the force of her climax. She shuddered and came back to earth slowly, opening her eyes sluggishly in time to see Ben poised above her. She grinned and accepted him as he slid into her body in one slow push that seemed to fill her completely. She reveled in the way his eyelids fluttered shut with a groan that she felt rock her soul. This was what it felt like to make love, she thought in a heated fog, the realization intensifying the physical sensations rioting through her body.

"Nora," he gasped her name, burying his face against the crook of her neck as he slid in and out with strong, powerful strokes. "Oh…"

He tensed and shuddered before collapsing against her, their hearts perfectly aligned and beating wildly together, raining soft kisses along her collarbone before uttering a single word, "Amazing…"

He didn't know the half of it.

## CHAPTER SEVENTEEN

NORA WAS NEVER a cuddler, but as soon as Ben pulled her to him she curled against his body as if it was the most natural thing in the world, and simply enjoyed the feel of his skin against hers.

He kissed the back of her neck and she heard him inhale softly. "You have the most intoxicating smell," he murmured against the shell of her ear, causing her to shiver. "I can't quite describe it. It's just you and I can't seem to get enough of it."

She smiled. "Maybe I should bottle it and try to market it somehow."

He growled. "I don't like to share."

A tingle warmed her belly at his statement and she settled into her pillow, her eyes drifting shut. "Neither do I," she countered softly.

She was nearly asleep when his voice brought her back to consciousness. "What did you say?" she asked with a small yawn.

"Nothing. Go back to sleep."

There was something troubling about the timbre of his voice but she was too tired to rouse herself to find out. Whatever it was, it could wait until morning.

And then she dropped off into the most restful sleep she'd ever had.

EARLY THE NEXT MORNING Ben rose and made Nora breakfast while she slept. He didn't sleep very well and he wished he could blame his restless night on Nora's snoring but he couldn't. He loved the way her body curled into his in a completely trustful manner and he was racking his brains to find a way to extend their relationship into more than his short stay in Emmett's Mill would allow. Ben wasn't accustomed to wooing a woman and he didn't know where to start. But he'd find out, because he wasn't ready to let her go.

He hobbled to the bedroom with a laden tray just as she woke, stretching and making little noises like a sated cat after a bowl of cream, and he nearly dropped their breakfast on the floor.

"Good morning, sexy," he said, coming to set the tray before her. Her eyes widened and her gaze flew to his as he grinned. "Denver omelet, the sequel. This one you'll be able to eat."

"God, that smells good," she said, taking the fork and, without a hint of bashfulness, sectioned off a piece. She groaned when she popped the food into her mouth and speared another piece. "Perfect," she said with her cheeks full. "But you shouldn't be moving around so much. If Doc Hessle knew how much you were doing, he'd give you an earful," she admonished as Ben grabbed his own fork and followed suit. "But you are a fabulous cook. Of course, you probably know this, but I don't mind saying it again— you can cook for me anytime."

His gaze narrowed at the innocent comment and she stopped. "Did I say something wrong?" she asked.

"No. I'd make anything your heart desires," he answered honestly. "All you have to do is say yes."

"Say yes?" She swallowed with difficulty, her eyes widening. "What do you mean?"

"Nora, will you be my girlfriend?"

The light dimmed in her gaze and he realized his question hadn't been the one she'd been hoping for. She speared another bite and chewed slowly, careful to avoid his eyes. "Ben, we've already covered this topic."

"I didn't like the outcome," he said, watching her closely, noting her demeanor had changed and she'd returned to her naturally guarded state. The change disappointed him but he didn't give up. "Why not, Nora?" he pressed.

He read the hurt in her expression. "Because I refuse to start a relationship that has no hope of going further. It's pointless."

"Why?" he asked, frustration at her argument coloring his voice. "Who starts a relationship with the expectation that a walk down the aisle is inevitable? Wait, don't answer. Apparently too many, which explains the rampant divorce rate in California. That's the moment they come to their senses and realize they never should've tied the knot in the first place."

He got up from the bed and she pushed the tray away. Anger crept into her cheeks, dusting her face with hot spots of color. "And who starts a relationship with the knowledge that it's destined to go *nowhere?*"

"I can't believe a woman as highly educated as yourself is refusing to go into a relationship with a man whom you're clearly attracted to just because he doesn't want to get married!"

She swung her legs over the side of the bed

and jerked the bedsheets around her naked body. He only had a moment of regret in losing sight of her luscious figure before she was stomping past him with the ire of a woman scorned.

"Screw you, Hollister," she snapped, and he couldn't help the snarl that followed.

"If I remember correctly, that's exactly what you did last night and I didn't hear any complaints!"

She skewcred him with a glare before slamming the bedroom door. He quickly followed.

"Where are you going? You're naked!"

Nora glanced down at her body and her lips tightened as she realized she'd left her clothes behind. She would have to push past him to return to the bedroom, but he knew she'd rather walk on hot coals than go anywhere near him and for once he was glad. She wouldn't dare leave wearing only a bedsheet and he wasn't finished with the conversation.

He took a deep breath to cool his temper and tried again. "Nora, we're good together. We share a connection that makes the sex between us out of this world. We both enjoy each other's company. We're intellectually compatible and certainly compatible in bed—why won't you just give it a chance?"

Her eyes brightened suspiciously and he realized Nora was on the verge of tears. The urge to cradle her in his arms was strong, but not stronger than his need to hear her agree to give his way a shot. "Honey, I'm not like that other guy. I'll never lie to you and pretend to offer something I have no intention of sharing. Does that mean nothing? Why won't you give me a chance?"

Nora stiffened and glared. "Because you're worse."

"Worse? Worse than the guy who used you?" He took offense. "How? I've been nothing but honest with you from the very beginning. I desire you unlike any woman I've ever met and I know you feel the same about me. Why are you fighting it when it's so good?"

Her jaw hardened. "It's good for *you*, Ben. I've already told you it's not good for me. That's your problem. You're so accustomed to looking out for yourself you don't take the time to consider how someone else might feel." She tugged the sheet closer around her body. "And I'm not interested in your offer. Contrary to what you think, you're no different than Griffin. You just have a different way of asking for the same thing. You want me on your terms, no matter the cost to anyone else. I'll tell you what I told him. Whatever we had is over. Goodbye."

And then she did exactly what he didn't think she would and marched out the door.

NORA REFUSED to cry—at least that's what she told herself fiercely as tears stung the back of her eyes. She had a knack for picking the biggest jerks on the planet. If there were a market for such a talent, she'd be a millionaire. But no one wanted her gift—least of all her.

Her heart wailed as she drove, and she used the edge of the sheet still wrapped around her body to wipe at her nose. She should've stuck to her original plan and ignored him, but damn if he didn't worm his way back into her good graces. Manipulative lawyer scum, she wanted to scream, but her throat closed as another wave of sadness threatened to drown her. What was wrong with the men she was attracted to?

Bettina rumbled into Nora's driveway and kicked up a cloud of dust as she pulled in. Nearly tripping in her haste to get into the house, she yanked at the caught bedsheet and ran in, hating Ben, hating men, hating her inability to spot a decent man amongst the snakes curling around her.

BEN STARED IN SHOCK as Nora jumped into her battered truck and sped down the driveway. Spurred into action a second too late, he managed to get outside in time to eat a cloud of dust.

Stumbling into the house, he winced as his ankle protested the action. Once in the study he riffled through papers on his desk, looking for Nora's business card. Finding it, he grabbed the phone and dialed her cell phone. As he expected, it rang four times and then went to voice mail, which meant she'd just screened his call. He tried again. This time there was no ring, only voice mail, telling him she'd shut off her phone. Reaching for the business card, he read the address printed on it. Grabbing whatever clothes were within reaching distance, he threw them onto his body and scrambled to his car. This was not over—not by a long shot!

He stared down at his foot and weighed his options. He could kill himself trying to drive with this stupid cast. The manual transmission didn't lend itself to accommodating a crippled foot. Dammit! A crazy thought came to him and as he practically dragged himself back into the house to the office, he knew this idea was a long shot.

Pulling Nora's estimate from his desk, he

flipped through to the page listing her sub-contractors and found the contact number for Sammy Halvorsen. The guy didn't like him very much, but maybe luck was on his side. Ben could only hope.

"You want me to what?" Sammy asked incredulously once Ben got him on the line and explained the circumstances. "You're nuts."

"I can't drive and I have to talk to her." He tried a little harder to appeal to some sort of guy loyalty. "Have you ever met a woman that gets under your skin so bad that it goes beyond any pleasure or pain you've ever felt?"

There was a long pause on the other end, and Ben had the sinking feeling he'd banked on the wrong emotion until Sammy sighed and a forced chuckle followed.

"Man, do I ever. All right, here's the deal. I'll help you out, but you better not hurt her or you'll be dealing with me, got it?"

"Deal. Now hurry up and get over here. She's already got a ten minute head start on us."

AFTER A NAUSEATING half hour of navigating twisting country roads, Sammy pulled into

Nora's driveway and said he'd wait outside. "Good luck, city boy."

Ben accepted the dubious offer of luck and wondered if he'd ever earn a different nickname around this town. He made his way to the front door, giving it a sharp rap before entering the house.

"Nora?" he called out, going from room to room until he heard the faint sound of sniffling. An abrupt detour later, he found Nora in the bedroom, curled on her side and crying into her pillow. The sight tore at his heart. He swallowed the lump in his throat and said, "Please come talk to me. I don't want to end this on such a bad note."

She lifted her head, shocked to see him standing there. "What are you doing here? How did you—"

"I talked Sammy into bringing me," he answered.

She narrowed her gaze and snorted. "Some best friend he is," she added with a watery sniff. "If you've come to retrieve your bedsheet, I threw it in the trash."

Startled, he said, "You threw it in the trash?"

"I was all out of lighter fluid," she retorted.

Right. Focus. "Okay, you're mad. I get that."

She popped up, indignation flashing in

her eyes. "Mad? I'm more than mad, you idiot. I'm hurt."

Chagrined, he tried again. "I'm sorry. I didn't mean to hurt you. I was trying *not* to hurt you."

She made a face. "Well you're terrible at it."

"I know. I have a talent for honing in on someone's vulnerable spots and poking at them. I've been trying to change…that's why I wanted to open my own firm. I'm tired of being the ruthless bastard I'm known as."

She wiped at her tears, still listening. That gave him courage to continue. "Nora…when my last girlfriend broke up with me, I swore I wouldn't get into another relationship unless she knew from the start that I wasn't the kind of man who wanted marriage and kids. I didn't tell my last girlfriend and we ended a relationship that I thought was pretty good, until I realized after a year she was waiting for me to pop the question. I didn't want to hurt you like that."

She swallowed and her expression looked wounded, not for herself this time but for him. "My parents were married for forty-seven years before my mom died of pancreatic cancer. I thought my dad was going to climb into the grave with her he loved her so much. My sister Tasha and her husband,

Josh, were high-school sweethearts who never stopped loving each other and ended up married almost twenty years later, still so in love it hurts to look at them. My other sister, Natalie, is married to a man who thinks the sun rises and sets in her smile and doesn't mind that she's a worrier and wound too tight. Love is real, Ben. It's out there. Has it ever occurred to you that what you see is only a skewed version?"

Ben's lips clenched together and his heart thumped painfully against his chest. She didn't see the ugliness he saw every day. "What if you're wrong, Nora? What if what *I* see is the norm and not the exception? It's a scientific fact that love is a chemical reaction in the brain that can be simulated in a lab. How romantic is that? Love can be induced in lab monkeys, but that's not something we want to put on a greeting card, now is it?"

She drew back in shock and he cursed under his breath, hating that she'd hit a nerve. "Nora, once my parents were happy. I have good memories of going to the park for picnics, boating on a Sunday afternoon, and my mother teaching me how to ride my horse. But they're overshadowed by the bad memories of a marriage disintegrating before my eyes as two people who were supposed to love each other 'till death do us part' started their own War of the Roses. I refuse to go through that myself. It's better to stop while you're ahead."

"Life without love isn't worth living," she said sadly.

"That's your opinion," he retorted coldly. "And a naive one at that. Contrary to what you may believe, love doesn't make the world go round—money does. And we all know there's nothing warm and fuzzy about the pursuit thereof."

She looked at him reproachfully, but he refused to give in to the pull of regret. Perhaps she was right. They had no future. He was stupid to have come hoping otherwise. He should let her go, both professionally and personally.

But she beat him to it and he didn't like the sound—or feel of it.

"Ben, I quit. You're going to need to find someone else to finish the job. I'm sorry. I've never quit a job before, but I can't work with you there. It's too hard."

He swallowed at the quiet anguish in her voice, knowing how difficult it would have been for Nora to admit such vulnerability and his opinion of himself took a nosedive.

"Please don't quit," he said, despite her

protests. "It's not necessary. I'll leave in the morning. You can finish the landscaping without me around. I'll leave a check on the hallway table."

"Ben, you don't have to leave. It would be easier to replace me. Besides, you can't leave yet. You can't even drive. Who will take care of you?"

Ben chuckled blackly. "Nora, don't be ridiculous. Your work is almost finished. It would be twice as expensive to hire someone new, and if I can pay you to take care of me, I can find someone else to do it for a short while."

He didn't mean to make it sound as if she was easily replaced, but the pain in his chest made it hard to temper his words.

"Sounds like you have everything figured out," she said icily. "Your ride is waiting."

In other words: get the hell out.

He stiffened and with as much dignity as a man on crutches could maintain, he walked out.

What he didn't say but certainly believed was that Nora would be impossible to replace in his life. He wouldn't even try.

He climbed into the truck and Sammy regarded him curiously. "Didn't go well?" he surmised.

"You could say that," Ben answered.

Sammy put the truck in Reverse and chuckled lightly.

Ben gave him a sharp look. "What's so funny?"

"Life. You never know when it's going to throw a curveball."

Ben snorted. "This is no curveball—it's a goddamn train wreck."

## CHAPTER EIGHTEEN

THE NEXT DAY Nora went to Ben's and found his car gone and a fat check on the hallway table just as he'd promised. Her immediate thought was how he'd managed to drive the car, but figured he'd paid someone to take him back to the city. As he said, he could probably find anyone for the right price. Forgoing the check, she wiped at her eyes and wandered the house, feeling her heart break for his absence. Hopefully his new driver cost him more than an arm and a leg— a kidney, perhaps.

It was several minutes before she could focus on the day ahead. Ben was right about the job—it was nearly finished and it was silly to hire someone else. Plus, for selfish reasons, she hated the idea of someone else coming in and putting their mark on her work, so she put her heart on hold and her head on track. This was something into which she could pour her energy.

Nora lost herself in planting rows of cheery yellow spring primrose and orange marigolds along the side of the house, when the sound of a car caught her attention. Pausing long enough to see if it was Ben, she returned to her planting when she saw it was not.

"I've been calling your cell and it's just going straight to voice mail," Sammy complained as he strode to her. "What gives?"

She shrugged. "Didn't feel like talking. Especially to you," she added pointedly.

"All right. I'll take that hit because I drove him to you, but he sounded so pitiful he tugged at my heartstrings."

"I didn't know you had heartstrings to pull," she said, still angry and feeling betrayed. "What do you want? Like I said, I don't really feel like talking."

He did a double take. "Since when? I believe Nora Simmons not feeling like talking is the fifth sign of the apocalypse."

Nora didn't have the will to chuckle at Sammy's joke. "What did you need, Sammy?"

He came to squat beside her, squinting against the sun. "I haven't talked to you in a while and needed a girl's perspective, but it doesn't look like you're up to dispensing advice. Listen, I'm sorry that city boy broke your heart. I thought, maybe, I don't know, there might be something between you guys. I thought you might be in love with him and were just too stubborn to admit it."

"So you sold me out on the premise of love?" she asked but she'd lost some of her fire. "Whatever. It doesn't matter. He's gone."

"So...good riddance, right?"

She looked at Sammy sharply and he lifted his hands in defense. "Don't bite my head off, just following your lead. What happened?"

She sighed and wiped her brow with her wrist before sitting back on her haunches. "You were right. I fell in love with him. Stupid me, huh?"

Sammy sobered and gestured toward the house. "He got beer in his fridge?" She nodded and he helped her up. "Then let's go snag a few. You and I've got a lot of catching up to do."

Nora smiled, grateful for a friend as solid as Sammy and followed him into the house.

Cracking open two dark import beers, Sammy and Nora found themselves back outside on the porch, commandeering chairs they found in a shed.

Sammy dusted hers off, saying, "A little dirt never hurt anyone. C'mon, let's talk."

"There's nothing to talk about, Sammy. He practically warned me at every turn not to fall in love with him because he didn't believe in love or marriage, and I did it anyway. What can I say? I'm an idiot."

"No, you're not. You're a closet romantic," Sammy countered. "Always have been. It's just that most people don't dig hard enough to reach that soft underbelly of yours. Unfortunately, the two that have, happened to poke at you with a sharp stick."

She exhaled. "All right, wise one…enough."

"Well, all I'm trying to say is there's nothing wrong with you. If this man of yours is too dumb to see what's right in front of him, that's his problem. And that other guy, what was his name? Grissom? Grendel? Gristle—"

"*Griffin.*"

"Whatever. He was just a jackass and you're better off without him."

"I know. But I thought Ben was different. I really did." She refrained from describing the connection she'd shared with Ben, it only made her feel worse. "It's going to be hard letting him go."

*And this house,* she realized. It had long ago started to feel like her home and the thought of someone else walking the halls and enjoying her koi pond made her want to weep.

Stupidly she'd started to picture the halls filled with family—her sisters and their children—maybe her own. She tipped the beer back and closed her eyes against the tears threatening to fall.

Sammy wisely remained silent and she struggled to get a grip, refocusing on what was important. She cleared her throat, but a catch remained in her voice as she said, "Ben paid me. I'll cut you a check tomorrow for the backhoe work."

He waved her away. "I know you're good for it. Whenever."

She smiled her gratitude. He instinctively knew she was putting off cashing that check. It was illogical, but somehow she thought if she didn't cash the check, Ben's leaving wasn't real. That he'd have to return at some point. But the very fact that she was clinging to such a ridiculous hope made her angry at herself.

Finishing the rest of her beer, she handed Sammy the empty bottle and stood. "Break's over. I have new sod coming tomorrow. If you're available, I could use an extra back."

"You got it, friend. Need anything else? Like someone to pummel that ex-boyfriend of yours?"

Her smile was brief. "He wasn't my boy-friend."

He wasn't anything.

BY THE TIME Sammy showed up the next morning, Nora had been at the job for two hours. She hadn't been able to sleep and didn't see the point of lying in bed staring at the ceiling when there was work to be done. Her cell phone remained off and she was afraid of turning it back on. What if he called? Worse, what if he didn't? Either way it was safer to keep it off.

Sweat poured down her back and soaked the waistband of her jeans but she didn't stop. Laying sod was backbreaking work but she welcomed the physical exhaustion. Her muscles screamed as she pulled another layer of sod from the pile and laid it into place, covering the freshly installed sprin-kler system in neat rectangles.

Sammy sensed she was in a rhythm and didn't start the morning with chatter. They worked side by side like robots until noon and the entire lawn was done. It looked glorious, but Nora wasn't sitting back to admire her work. The gazebo was also arriving today and she needed to clear the area so they could carry it in. She also had to fill the koi pond and drop in the fish—they were waiting in a special container, but couldn't stay there long.

Nora and Sammy were hefting the gazebo into place when a Honda Accord drove into the driveway. Nora glanced up and looked to Sammy. He broke into a nervous grin and gestured for the driver to come over.

"Who's that?" she asked, though she had a fair idea and she wasn't in the mood to entertain guests.

"Take a break," he suggested, but Nora waved him away. "C'mon, I want you to meet someone."

"We've already met, remember?" Nora said sourly, not caring that she sounded like a shrew. It was fitting. She felt like one. "Go ahead, I can finish."

"Nora, it's important to me," he said, his suddenly earnest tone catching her ear. "I need you guys to get off on the right foot." He gestured to the woman getting out of the car. "Dana, come on over. Watch the grass, though, it's new."

Dana, the bossy paramedic, made her way over to them and for a second the two women simply regarded each other warily, as if waiting to see if defensive maneuvers were warranted. Finally, Dana extended her hand to Nora. "We haven't been formally introduced, but I've heard a lot about you."

Nora shook her hand. "Don't believe everything you hear," she said, shrugging. "Then again, maybe you should. Half of it's right, the other half's wrong but you never know which is which."

"Samuel speaks very highly of you," she said, smiling at Sammy.

Nora angled a look at Sammy. *Samuel?* He grinned sheepishly. *So that's how it is.* "Nice to meet you. Sorry about my behavior earlier. I was under a lot of stress that day with my client falling down a hill and nearly killing himself. He wore the wrong shoes," she said as if that explained it all.

"Nora, we wanted to tell you something in person because the news we have just doesn't seem right to say over the phone but the last few days you've been hard to track down," Sammy said, and Nora blushed, knowing exactly what she'd been doing. Dana slipped her hand into Sammy's and Nora got a queasy feeling. *Not now*, she wanted to groan, but Sammy was beaming like a blooming idiot. "We're getting married."

"You and her?" she asked, cringing seconds later when she realized how rude that sounded, but she was tired and cranky and even on the best of days hardly tactful.

Dana stiffened but Sammy rushed to smooth things over. "Try to contain your joy. It's damn near contagious. C'mon, usually congratulations are in order."

Inexplicably Nora's eyes watered and she nodded, ashamed of herself for feeling so bitter inside when her best friend was sharing the happiest moment of his life with her. "Congratulations, Sammy, Dana. I hope you're very happy together and it's not just a chemical reaction in the brain!"

Spinning on her heel she ran into the safety of the house and buried her face in Ben's pillow, inhaling his lingering scent and hating that she missed him and was tempted to agree to any term he liked as long as he came back to her. Pathetic, but true. God help her, how pathetic.

BEN CLOSED his briefcase and prepared to leave the courtroom but his client, Ed Wallace, was spitting mad.

"You rotten bastard, she took half my estate!" he said, spittle flying from his mouth to land on his expensive tie. Wallace glanced around and readjusted his suit before continuing in a malevolent hiss. "I'll see you out of a job by the end of the day for your incompetence. By the time I'm through, you won't be able to give legal advice at a free clinic. Mark my words, Hollister. You're career is *over*."

Ben ignored the malice in Ed's voice. "I told you to settle. I'm not a miracle worker. You should've heeded my advice before she wised up. Better luck next time."

"If you think it's a coincidence that she found out about my account in the Cayman Islands, you're royally screwed in the head. I'll have you disbarred for sharing confidential information with the enemy," Ed vowed, nearly vibrating with anger, but Ben could care less. He felt oddly liberated despite the fact that Ed Wallace would most assuredly end his legal career in the Bay Area. He'd think about that later.

He moved past Ed and walked over to opposing counsel, surprising both the former Mrs. Wallace and her attorney. He shook her attorney's hand and offered a smile that was more relieved than professional though he hoped they saw only the latter. "Don't waste a moment worrying about Ed. Men like him always land on their feet. Good luck."

Mrs. Wallace met his gaze and smiled tremulously, communicating she was grateful but if she knew the identity of the man who'd provided her the confidential information she needed to win, she'd never tell.

He inclined his head and left.

Ben was halfway to his office when he spotted the lithe figure of Elise Birkeland standing beside one of the senior partners. He offered a wave and cloistered himself inside.

Isaac Franklin, senior partner of the firm, walked in unannounced, but Ben wasn't surprised. "Isaac, what can I do for you?" he asked congenially, steepling his fingers as he waited. *This is the part where I'm fired,* he thought to himself.

"Ed Wallace is ranting and raving about how you sabotaged his case. Is this true?" Isaac asked point-blank.

Ben considered his answer and opted for a variation of the truth. "I told him to settle. He refused. The man's a greedy bastard and he got what he deserved."

"It's not our job to determine morality. It's our job to win," Isaac reminded him, his gaze shrewd. "And you didn't answer my question. Is there any validity to Ed's claim?"

He looked Isaac straight in the eye and

imagined saying yes, that he'd deliberately offered information that would sink his client, but he wasn't stupid. "No." He leaned back in his chair. "You and I both know Ed Wallace is stupid and prone to bragging. He could've blabbed about his offshore account to the tart he's seeing or any other person who might've been impressed by that sort of thing." He shrugged. "I did the best I could with what I had to work with."

Isaac grunted an acknowledgment. "You've a point. We'll get the bill out quickly before he starts moving money around. Good job, Benjamin. It was a tough case but in light of the circumstances, I don't think anyone else could've done better."

Ben let the praise bounce off him, knowing it meant nothing. Next week, he'd get another case just like this one and he'd be expected to win, no matter the cost.

Closing his eyes, he tried to savor the look on Mrs. Wallace's face when the judge ruled in her favor, but Elise's entrance interrupted him.

Her svelte beauty did nothing to arouse him, which he noted was probably a travesty in some neck of the world, but it was true. The only woman that turned his head was miles away and out of reach.

"You were missed, darling," Elise said, coming to sit on the corner of his desk, her expensive couture suit smelling of money and power. Her ice-blue eyes were watching him closely. "Are you healed from your injury?"

"Just a twinge now and then."

"So glad to hear of it. It must've been dreadful tucked away in that mountain town with your country girl," she mused. "So nice to be back in civilization, yes?"

Yeah. What's not to miss about bumper-to-bumper traffic, graffiti and crazy people talking to themselves? "There were some things I enjoyed about the mountains," he admitted. Like Nora. Waking up with her in his arms, listening to her snore, even arguing.

She waved away his answer. "Pooh on that. Clean air, quaint lifestyles, too *Green Acres* for the likes of us. We thrive on what the city can provide. Come to the theater with me tonight. I have box seats and Isaac has made other plans."

"So you're seeing Isaac now?" he asked and she lifted one shoulder in a delicate shrug.

"He amuses me. For the time being. You know how it goes. He's here today, perhaps not tomorrow. I don't waste time chasing one man when there are so many more out there to choose from." She tapped his desk, demanding his attention. "Come with me, yes?"

"Another time," he suggested, though they both knew he wouldn't.

She sighed and rose from his desk. "Go back to your country girl," she directed with an air of bored indifference. "She has sucked all the fun out of you."

He chuckled at Elise's pique. She would forget about him within seconds; her interest in anything was fleeting. But she'd managed to zero in on one essential truth—Nora had done something to him. He was different. And the change might just be the best thing that had ever happened to him.

# CHAPTER NINETEEN

"NORA," GUSHED HER SISTERS as they surveyed the finished grounds. "God, it's gorgeous!"

Nora smiled with pleasure at her sisters' praise and agreed silently. The finished yard was a dream. The koi were swimming in their new habitat, their flashes of brilliant color peeking out from beneath giant floating lily pads, and the fountain gurgled as if chortling with delight over its new polished and buffed exterior.

The lawn extended around the house with an arbor leading to Nora's herb garden, and the air was sweet and fragrant with the varied flowers and foliage. They were right; it was gorgeous.

Yet her heart felt like lead in her chest. Ben was not here to enjoy it with her. She'd given up hope that he'd at least call, and she expected the last she'd hear from him would be when he received her final invoice and cut the check for the expenses. Leaving her sisters to explore the grounds, she wound her way down the newly constructed pathway to the creek and found a place to sit beside the water.

The blackberry bushes were beginning to bloom, and come summer they'd be bursting with fresh berries, though it was likely only the wildlife would enjoy them.

The creek ran swiftly, still swollen from the winter runoff coming off the mountain but Nora was safe in her spot. It wasn't far from here where she first met Ben. Drawing her knees against her chest, she sank into her sorrow and wondered if she'd ever be able to look at this creek again without wanting to burst into a horrible display of girlie tears.

"I rather like the stairs after all," a voice said behind her. She whirled and saw Ben, of all people, standing on the last step, smiling, cast free. "It seems you were right after all."

She wiped at her eyes and stood stiffly. "What are you talking about?" she asked, trying not to notice how her heart had tripled its beat. "What are you doing here? I would've mailed the key back to you if that's what you're worried about."

"Now, where would the sense in that be?" he chided her, further confusing her and setting her nerves on edge.

"Have you lost your mind or started doing hallucinogenic drugs? You're not making any sense. Of course you need your spare key." Unless the house had already sold. She faltered, her dreams crashed and burned. She blinked back tears. "What's going on?"

He stepped forward and came within touching distance. She couldn't retreat without landing in the water. She glared at him for invading her space. "It seems you were right and I was wrong about a number of things," he began. "Starting with the stairway, herb garden and koi pond. The house looks fabulous."

She relaxed only a little. "Anything else?" Damn, was that her voice that sounded so hopeful?

"Just this…" His voice softened and her heart did a strange little skip as he pulled her to him, his gaze caressing her face. "Love *is* more than a chemical reaction. It's real and it's been with me ever since I left this place."

"Ben, if this is some kind of joke, I'm not laughing."

"I hope to God you don't think this is a joke because I'm about to ask you to spend the rest of your life with me. I've quit my job at Franklin, Mills & Donovan, and I'm going to open up shop here, in Emmett's Mill. I figure this town could use someone to fill my grandfather's shoes and I know I'm the only man for the job. I even parked the Beemer and bought my own car. An SUV with monster tires in case it snows around here."

She gasped. "Are you serious?"

He gave her a look that melted her heart. "I've never been more serious in my life. Will you make an honest man out of me and promise to tell me when I'm being a jackass until the day I die?"

Nora beamed, unable to believe what was happening. She wrapped her arms around his neck as pure joy cascaded through her body. "Only if you promise to love me every single day of those years together."

"Is that a yes?" he asked a bit anxiously, and she answered him with a kiss.

"Yes, Benjamin Scott Hollister III," she said against his mouth. "Yes, yes and God, yes!"

## EPILOGUE

"A WEDDING IN September?" Natalie groaned. "It'll be so hot. Why not next April? What's the rush?"

Nora sent a secret smile to Ben and his gaze settled on her stomach. No one knew yet, but she was three months pregnant and if they didn't tie the knot soon, her father would be ordering a shotgun wedding.

Tasha smiled and reached over to pick up Justin Cole from his swing. "I think he's teething, Nat. He's drooled all over his front," she observed, accepting a clean onesie from Natalie so his auntie could change him.

Gerald was bending Ben's ear about something that had him riled and was no doubt pestering him for legal advice and Josh and Evan, her brothers-in-law were exclaiming over Nora's herb garden and asking if she could help them plant their own.

"Smell this oregano," Evan said, pushing the herb right under Natalie's nose until she sneezed. "Can you imagine a spaghetti sauce with some of this in it?"

She waved it away from her nose. "Sounds great." When Evan wandered off to finish his exploration, Natalie leaned over to Nora and whispered, "No oregano. I'm allergic."

Nora smiled, her heart full to bursting. She'd never seen herself as the type to cherish home and hearth like some people, but until she had something worth cherishing herself, she'd never known what she'd been missing.

She had the house she'd always wanted, but better than that, she was living the dream she never truly knew she wanted until it had almost been taken from her.

She let her hand slide surreptitiously to her still-flat stomach and her gaze returned to her soon-to-be husband. Now she knew.

And life was great.

\* \* \* \* \*

Look for LAST WOLF WATCHING
by Rhyannon Byrd—the exciting
conclusion in the
BLOODRUNNERS miniseries
from Silhouette Nocturne.

Follow Michaela and Brody on their
fierce journey to find the truth and face the
demons from the past, as they reach the
heart of the battle between
the Runners and the rogues.

Here is a sneak preview of book three,
LAST WOLF WATCHING.

Michaela squinted, struggling to see through the impenetrable darkness. Everyone looked toward the Elders, but she knew Brody Carter still watched her. Michaela could feel the power of his gaze. Its heat. Its strength. And something that felt strangely like anger, though he had no reason to have any emotion toward her. Strangers from different worlds, brought together beneath the heavy silver moon on a night made for hell itself. That was their only connection.

The second she finished that thought, she knew it was a lie. But she couldn't deal with it now. Not tonight. Not when her whole world balanced on the edge of destruction.

Willing her backbone to keep her upright, Michaela Doucet focused on the towering blaze of a roaring bonfire that rose from the far side of the clearing, its orange flames burning with maniacal zeal against the inky black curtain of the night. Many of the Lycans had already shifted into their preternatural shapes, their fur-covered bodies standing like monstrous shadows at the edges of the forest as they waited with restless expectancy for her brother.

Her nineteen-year-old brother, Max, had been attacked by a rogue werewolf—a Lycan who preyed upon humans for food. Max had been bitten in the attack, which meant he was no longer human, but a breed of creature that existed between the two worlds of man and beast, much like the Bloodrunners themselves.

The Elders parted, and two hulking shapes emerged from the trees. In their wolf forms, the Lycans stood over seven feet tall, their legs bent at an odd angle as they stalked forward. They each held a thick chain that had been wound around their inside wrists, the twin lengths leading back into the shadows. The Lycans had taken no more han a few steps when they jerked on the chains, and her brother appeared.

Bound like an animal.

Biting at her trembling lower lip, she glanced left, then right, surprised to see that others had joined her. Now the Bloodrunners and their family and friends stood as a united force against the Silvercrest pack, which had yet to accept the fact that something sinister was eating away at its foundation—something that would rip down the protective walls that separated their world from the humans'. It occurred to Michaela that loyalties were being announced tonight—a separation made between those who would stand with the Runners in their fight against the rogues and those who blindly supported the pack's refusal to face reality. But all she could focus on was her brother. Max looked so hurt…so terrified.

"Leave him alone," she screamed, her soft-soled, black satin slip-ons struggling for purchase in the damp earth as she rushed toward Max, only to find herself lifted off the ground when a hard, heavily muscled arm clamped around her waist from behind, pulling her clear off her feet. "Damn it, let me down!" she snarled, unable to take her eyes off her brother as the golden-eyed Lycan kicked him.

Mindless with heartache and rage, Michaela clawed at the arm holding her, kicking her heels against whatever part of her captor's legs she could reach. "Stop it," a deep, husky voice grunted in her ear. "You're not helping him by losing it. I give you my word he'll survive the ceremony, but you have to keep it together."

"Nooooo!" she screamed, too hysterical to listen to reason. "You're monsters! All of you! Look what you've done to him! How dare you! *How dare you!*"

The arm tightened with a powerful flex of muscle, cinching her waist. Her breath sucked in on a sharp, wailing gasp.

"Shut up before you get both yourself and your brother killed. I will *not* let that happen. Do you understand me?" her captor growled, shaking her so hard that her teeth clicked together. "Do you understand me, Doucet?"

"Damn it," she cried, stricken as she watched one of the guards grab Max by his hair. Around them Lycans huffed and growled as they watched the spectacle, while others outright howled for the show to begin.

"That's enough!" the voice seethed in her ear. "They'll tear you apart before you even reach him, and I'll be damned if I'm going to stand here and watch you die."

Suddenly, through the haze of fear and agony and outrage in her mind, she finally recognized who'd caught her. *Brody.*

He held her in his arms, her body locked against his powerful form, her back to the burning heat of his chest. A low, keening sound of anguish tore through her, and her head dropped forward as hoarse sobs of pain ripped from her throat. "Let me go. I have to help him. *Please,*" she begged brokenly, knowing only that she needed to get to Max. "Let me go, Brody."

He muttered something against her hair, his breath warm against her scalp, and Michaela could have sworn it was a single word.... But she must have heard wrong. She was too upset. Too furious. Too terrified. She must be out of her mind.

Because it sounded as if he'd quietly snarled the word *never.*

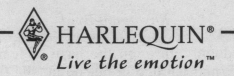

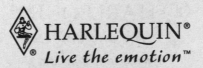

# HARLEQUIN®
# INTRIGUE®

## EATHTAKING ROMANTIC SUSPENSE

hared dangers and passions lead to electrifying
romance and heart-stopping suspense!

Every month, you'll meet six new heroes
who are guaranteed to make your spine tingle
and your pulse pound. With them you'll enter
nto the exciting world of Harlequin Intrigue—
where your life is on the line
and so is your heart!

## THAT'S INTRIGUE—
## ROMANTIC SUSPENSE
## AT ITS BEST!

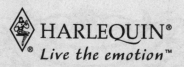

## HARLEQUIN®
### *Live the emotion*™

## Harlequin® Historical
### Historical Romantic Adventure!

*Imagine a time of chivalrous knights and unconventional ladies, roguish rakes and impetuous heiresses, rugged cowboys and spirited frontierswomen— these rich and vivid tales will capture your imagination!*

*Harlequin Historical . . . they're too good to miss!*

# HARLEQUIN®
## *Presents*®

**The world's bestselling romance series...
the series that brings you your favorite authors,
month after month:**

Helen Bianchin...Emma Darcy
Lynne Graham...Penny Jordan
Miranda Lee...Sandra Marton
Anne Mather...Carole Mortimer
Susan Napier...Michelle Reid

**and many more uniquely talented authors!**

Wealthy, powerful, gorgeous men...
Women who have feelings just like your own...
The stories you love, set in exotic, glamorous locations...

# HARLEQUIN®
## *Presents*®

**Seduction and Passion Guaranteed!**

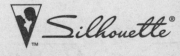